STRANGE EPIPHANIES

Strange Epiphanies

by

Peter Bell

Swan River Press
Dublin, Ireland
MMXXI

Strange Epiphanies
by Peter Bell

Published by
Swan River Press
Dublin, Ireland
in September, MMXXI

www.swanriverpress.ie
brian@swanriverpress.ie

Cover design by Meggan Kehrli
from "Melmerby" (2009) by R. B. Russell

Set in Garamond by Steve J. Shaw

ISBN 978-1-78380-748-2

Swan River Press published
a limited edition hardback of
Strange Epiphanies in April 2012.

Contents

✕

Introduction

When I first decided to start publishing, I made a short list of authors I wanted to work with. Peter Bell was at the top of that list, and the resulting publication was the first Haunted Histories booklet, *On the Apparitions at Gray's Court* (2006). The story is set in Peter's adopted hometown of York (Peter himself being a native of Liverpool). I have fond memories of visiting York over a decade ago while there on holiday. This was about a year before I relocated to my current hometown of Rathmines in Dublin, Ireland. I remember vividly now walking along the reedy banks of the River Ouse, passing into the city centre through one of the great stone gateways, and standing atop the medieval city wall that to this day still defends the essence of York from the outside world. And of course the lazy-leaning, timber-framed buildings of the Shambles, the city's old meat market, frozen in their lurching angles of slow collapse. A walk down the Shambles is a walk down a street that's not quite real, like something out of Murnau's expressionist nightmares, reality's architecture skewed and rearranged. And then, of course, there's Gray's Court.

Even though I never visited Gray's Court on that trip, I now have the distinct impression that I had, thanks to Peter's story. I am—or at least feel I am—well familiar with its stone-tiled undercroft, panelled wooden staircase, dust-moted halls, and plain leaded windows ("with some decorative, though unremarkable, stained glass"). Such details can be disarming and can even foster a cautious sense of comfort. But there's always something more to it, isn't there? What makes Gray's Court work so well is Peter's ability to evoke the building's *genius loci*. And by that I don't simply mean atmosphere, but rather its very demeanour. The actual spirit of place:

> There are numerous corners where the sun scarcely penetrates, though the intermittent passage of its beams throughout the day, glancing through the dust-motes in the various rooms, affords a pleasing contrast to the many shadows, creating odd angles of light and shade where shapes can seem to move. After dark, the dimly lit rooms and passageways echo with the sound of unseen footsteps; whilst entering the building late at night, reaching out to find the light switches, proceeding up the stairways and along the labyrinthine passages can be an unnerving experience . . .

It chills me to think of Gray's Court even now because in my "memories", false though they may be, I wander and explore those lonely halls alone. You should track down a copy of this story for yourself and read it. You'll see what I mean. But my point here is this: it's Peter's keen sense of place—his gift in conjuring those impressions on the page—that's what makes his stories work. And that includes the stories in the volume you're holding right now.

It's when we go on holiday that the spirit of place often seems magnified. We notice things that we otherwise might pass over, such as routines or familiarities that we take for granted, even come to rely upon. But when we're in an alien place, all that changes. Small, innocuous details can become oddly conspicuous and sometimes even sinister in their discordance with our expectations.

You may not be surprised, then, to learn that many of Peter's stories feature people on "holiday", at least holidays of sorts—people who voluntarily leave behind the comforts and familiarities of their daily lives; people who flee to places that might offer comfort, maybe even enlightenment, but are ultimately unfamiliar and loaded with potential for strangeness and *true* discovery.

In "Resurrection" we overnight in a bed and breakfast called "The Ferns" in the rural community of Greendale (sounds harmless enough, right?); "M.E.F." takes us to the isolated island of Iona in western Scotland and its confusing, desolate moorlands; in "The Light of the World" we visit, perhaps simultaneously, the desolate Blengdale Moors in western Cumbria, and the ancient walled town of Città di Castello in an equally remote part of Italy; we return to the rough scenery of the outer Hebrides in "An American Writer's Cottage"; both "Inheritance", set in a small town in Germany, and "Nostalgia, Death and Melancholy", set on the Isle of Man, explore the interior landscapes of obfuscated memories of youth; and "A Midsummer Ramble in the Carpathians" takes us on two separate journeys through the southern borderlands of Transylvania—first through a "lost" travel manuscript by Victorian author Amelia B. Edwards, and then alongside Julia P. Flint, "dealer in antiquarian books and maps", as she retraces the steps of Miss Edwards into the howling wilderness.

Peter Bell will be your guide to each of these less familiar places. And in each story he'll scratch beneath the top soil to unearth the true *genius loci*—the often unsettling spirit of place—and show its effects on those who tread these exposed surfaces. Landscapes that, with each turn, Peter gently skews and rearranges into something resembling nightmare.

But these stories are neither ghost stories nor strange tales. Their bent is something else entirely. These are stories of revelation, and while this notion of revelation might at first suggest an air of mystical enlightenment or of awe, we must always remember that not all revelations are welcome ones. These stories are strange epiphanies.

Brian J. Showers
Amsterdam, Holland
4 February 2012

Strange Epiphanies

In affectionate memory

MARCIA

"Since not again can I be with you life with life,
I would be with you as star with distant star,
As drop of water in the one bright bitter sea."

– Kathleen Raine, "Message to Gavin"

Resurrection

*"And my heart laughed with joy
To know the death I must die"*

– Kathleen Raine, *"Night Sky"*

Amanda first glimpsed the house from the miniature
steam train that bore her to her destination in
Greendale. It was a mystery house, of the kind she
had read about so often as a child in the "Famous Five"
stories of Enid Blyton: a substantial, well-proportioned
villa, built of red brick with red-tiled roof and ornamental
wooden gables; it looked as if it had been constructed in
the 1920s by some retiring entrepreneur from Lancashire.
Above the grand front porch was a covered balcony guarded
by an ornate balustrade, but it was impossible to tell if the
window set deep within the recess fronted a bedroom or a
landing. There was a figure standing at the balustrade; it
looked like a young woman with long fair hair. If it were a
bedroom, Amanda laughed nervously to herself, it would
be a creepy place to have to spend the night.

Amanda was undertaking this short holiday in the
month of May as a last ditch effort to expel the demons
of depression that had been her companions for the past
eighteen months. It was ironic that she, a psychiatrist of
some distinction, should so far have been unable to unlock
the prison door of mental breakdown. The advice of the

3

various doctors she could see right through; she knew too much, they said, shaking their heads. The initial grudging sympathy of her sister, Claire, had swiftly yielded to frustration, anger and undeserved harsh words: if only she were married, said Claire, and had children to care for, she wouldn't have time to be neurotic. But Amanda was not amongst those who believed children had been put on earth trailing clouds of glory. Even now, as the train carried her further and further into the heart of solitude, there were two of them squabbling noisily further down the coach, and she could hear somewhere the irritating mewling of a newborn baby. The tiny locomotive was chugging resolutely ahead, its toy-town carriages rattling from side to side through a fairyland of yellow gorse and broom, bluebell woods and rampant rhododendrons. An odd sensation overcame Amanda, as if she were travelling back to the years of her own childhood.

The enchantment of the scenery on this mellow, breezy afternoon reached out to her. She was overwhelmed by a cold and contemplative melancholy, an aching poignancy. Vague memories of springtimes long ago flashed before her mind, briefly glimpsed then lost, like a mystic vision, a revelation just out of reach. Why was it that this fairest of the seasons, so redolent of new life and the promise of new beginnings, spoke to her so eloquently of transience and death? Already the engine, a little gasping dragon, was slowing down; and the guard, a stout middle-aged boy, was self-importantly standing up and calling out the name of the station. Sooner than expected she had arrived, and Amanda scolded herself for being so morbid.

She was the only person alighting, and the guard fussily assisted her to lift her two bags (she always travelled light) onto the low platform. Then, ceremoniously raising his hand to the driver and blowing his whistle, he leapt back on board. Amanda watched as the locomotive tooted shrilly on its own whistle and began to haul the trundling coaches on to their final resting place for that day somewhere in the distant heart of the valley. As the sound of its departure gradually faded, Amanda drank in the silence and solitude she had so long craved. She breathed deeply and gratefully of the cool evening air, listening to the vespers of the many birds, her awakening senses revelling in the scents of myriad blooms, soothing her like the gentlest mother's caress. She thought, with a dull aching pain, of her own mother, so recently deceased, last frail linkage to a past so unappreciated at the time, so glorious now in memory.

A steep narrow track led away from the station, but there were no direction signs; it looked, indeed, worryingly private. Amanda, who was fastidious in these things, hesitated; she did not wish to trespass. But there seemed no other way. She could always say, quite truthfully, that she was searching for somewhere called "The Ferns"—booked over the phone on the strength of a small advertisement in *The Lady*. The path climbed precipitously between honeysuckle-festooned hedges. There were occasional small gateways, side-entrances to the gardens of substantial houses glimpsed through luxuriant shrubberies. There were names on some: "Beech Howe", "Rockside", "Laurel Canyon"—but of "The Ferns" she could discern no sign. All around, spring was in abandon. Golden laburnum rain draped the path, its pungent odour mingling strangely with the honeysuckle sweetness. Clematis climbed wildly. Cherry trees dangled remnant blossoms over petal carpets. Aisles of bluebells flanked the verges, interspersed with the tattered pink flowers of ragged robin. Everywhere stretched a multicoloured tableau of rhododendron and azalea. And there were other blooms and scents, elusive and vaguely unsettling.

Abruptly she reached a natural elevation in the craggy landscape, revealing a surprising vista, eerie in its perfection. Undulating rocky gardens extended in every direction, their rainbow colours reflecting the pellucid evening light. Elegant old villas peered from hidden glades, flanked here and there by monkey puzzles, wellingtonias and less familiar conifers. Amanda idly wondered if she were near the mystery house, but either it was unrecognisable from a different angle or else it was obscured by trees. The architecture of the houses was different from anything she recalled having seen anywhere in the Lake District, with extensive use of reddish-stone and patterned wooden framing rather than the usual grey Cumberland slate; ornate red chimney pots stood in place of the columnar stacks beloved of Beatrix Potter. No doubt they simply bore the hallmark of the ruby-tinted quartz that swept down the western side of the Cumbrian mountains, but to Amanda it all added to the sense of a strange reality that she had felt ever since boarding the miniature train at Ravenglass.

The path curved sharply down reaching a broader lane, and suddenly, there before her, was the mystery house. At close quarters it looked even more forbidding than from the train, though in scale it had flattered to deceive. It was a pompous house, flaunting its *nouveau riche* Edwardian vulgarity, yet it was not enormous. Unkempt laurel loomed over the Art Deco metal railings obscuring the entrance, though the balcony was clearly visible. It had a wild rambling garden. She proceeded, and soon, through a gap in the hedge, she espied a grandiose porch. And inscribed in the red stone above it, in large decorated script, was the dwelling's name. Anxiety seized her. By some sixth sense Amanda knew what it would be. It read: "The Ferns".

Yet what was the alternative? It was probably too late to find other quarters. In any case it offended every instinct of her nature not to stick to a plan; Amanda had a horror of change. She chided herself for her irrationality. Wasn't superstition the product of neurosis? Two elaborate pairs of metal gates stood at the bottom of two curving drives that led up through the property, eventually meeting at the porch steps. She took the left of these (the right hand one looked as if it had fallen into disuse, choked as it was with weeds and saplings) and strode up to the impressive entrance. She regarded the shaded balcony with trepidation. Why was it that its enclosing red stone balustrade spoke to her not so much of protection as of confinement?

The outer door of the porch was open. Stepping inside she faced an inner door of stained glass. Not liking to enter uninvited, Amanda rapped on the glass and then, noticing an old fashioned handbell on the floor, rang it tentatively. As its chimes died away, from behind her in the garden a well-spoken female voice addressed her. The speaker managed to imbue her tone with challenge rather than invitation: "Can *I* be of any help?"

A woman in her sixties, an aureole of once black hair wreathing her high forehead, observed her with a steady penetrating gaze. She was dressed in expensive-looking clothes, much too young for her.

"Ah!" she declared, regarding Amanda's bags, "Miss Simkin." Without waiting for confirmation, she continued, "We've been expecting you. I'll get Mrs. Burke . . . our maid." She smiled patronisingly, "I'm Mrs. Cardownie, by the way." Without exactly appearing unfriendly, her manner was of someone who had far higher things to attend to than the arrival of a guest. It did not augur well for her stay and Amanda wondered if after all it had been a good idea to come away on a holiday when she was still clearly not feeling herself.

7

The next unnerving moment was the advent of Mrs. Burke, who had silently arrived on the threshold as Amanda's back was turned. Mrs. Cardownie's reference to a maid had conjured an image quite different from the grim-faced crone now tapping on her shoulder. Mrs. Burke could scarcely have been less than eighty. She was dressed in the mode of a Victorian servant, with black gown and white headpiece. She spoke in the broad dialect of western Cumberland, with an odd upward lilt towards the end of each phrase, unsmiling though not unwelcoming. Gripping Amanda's bags with manly strength she lurched unevenly ahead, bidding her to follow, talking with unceasing garrulity.

"I'll tek yer round th' downstairs first, miss. Have yer had a cup o' tea? I'll make a nice one for yer. Just put bags 'ere a minit."

She swayed towards a door on the left of the hall leading Amanda into a spacious room, brightly-lit by the evening sun. One corner extended into a deep bay window offering a pleasant panorama round the large leafy garden.

"I'll bring tea in a moment, miss, this bein' guests' lounge. Yer the only one stayin'. I'll be lookin' after yer, as Mrs. Cardownie—she's the mistress, like—is rit busy, what with the garden and these 'ere Mayday celebrations comin' up. Beltane, we call it. There's buks, miss, if yer want. Never bother with'em meself—eyes not so gud these days. Just wait 'ere, an' I'll tek yer bags up t' the room. A real nice one, at front."

She squinted awkwardly at Amanda. What passed for a smile flickered for an instant across the thin line of her mouth. It made Amanda feel uneasy. Mrs. Burke reminded her of a picture in an old book of fairy tales that had scared her so much as a child she had sealed the page with sticky-tape. But this was ridiculous. It was only nerves. A panic attack. She must pull herself together. Just what the doctors had being saying for months. She realised she was shaking.

Amanda watched the elderly servant twist her way out of the lounge, fascinated by the combination of agedness and agility. She certainly looked stronger than Amanda felt, though that was of course only nervous debility; it was amazing how the mental state impinged on the material. As her anxiety receded, she decided Mrs. Burke was probably all right, despite her somewhat fearsome appearance; a kind soul really, doing her best for the comfort of the guest, which was more than could be said about her ill-mannered hostess who was apparently too busy organising "celebrations". She wondered what these were. It had never occurred to her city mind that echoes of the old pagan carnivals still survived in these remote country villages, for wasn't that what Beltane was? She felt vaguely annoyed that she should have chosen for a weekend's solitude a place of rural revelry—though it struck her as odd that, on such a busy occasion, she should be the only guest in the house. No doubt Mrs. Burke would enlighten her. Of Mrs. Cardownie she had already formed a distinct dislike. Amanda reminded herself she should be less negative in judging people; it was important to make sure depression did not transform into paranoia.

Uneven footsteps announced the arrival of tea. Mrs. Burke, despite her oscillating gait, kept the tray on an even keel, spilling not a drop of the strong, dark, reviving brew that Amanda was soon sipping gratefully as the elderly servant prattled on without a break. There had been no need to ask any questions about the local festivities, as Mrs. Burke was expounding upon them eloquently; clearly her knowledge of the area and its customs was unsurpassed.

"Aye! It's termorrer's the big day. Ev'ry May. An' what a grand May 'tis this year, miss, with blooms I never seen like of since I were a girl. An' five new babies born already in the month. More'n the village's seen in so many years. There's fancy dress, an' games, an' folks all dressed up as animals. Horses, wolves, goats, cats."

As if on cue a large black cat padded into the room, leapt onto a favourite armchair and stared unblinking at Amanda. Mrs. Burke, oblivious to everything except her own enthusiasm, was warming to her theme. "Oh! It's grand. An' we've still got old Maypole on village green. There's folks as say that Good Queen Bess herself danced around it. An' a big ox roasted, and then fires up on moor, all night. Aye, they say yer can see'em right out on th' Irish Sea."

The more Amanda heard, the less she liked. An excuse for a night of drunken revels by the sound of it. She would have to make sure she didn't stay up too late tomorrow night. But as her intention was to take long walks in the day and go to bed early that should not prove a problem, though God knows how she'd sleep if the festivities extended to the vicinity of The Ferns. She kept nodding politely as her raconteur went on, enjoying the stimulation of the tea. Taking advantage of a rare pause in Mrs. Burke's harangue, she asked if there were nearby some inn where she might catch an evening meal.

Seamlessly, Mrs. Burke's conversation turned into a eulogy to the local hospitality. Apparently there were two establishments to be recommended. Nearest was the Victoria Inn, and a little further away going out of the village was The Green Man.

"Victoria does a nice bar meal, miss, but gets a bit crowded from the camp site up th' valley, like. But The Green Man, now there's a real classy place, with a proper dinin' room and game on menu ev'ry night. An' yer can get bar meals if yer prefer. That's where locals go."

It was easily decided. The thought of dining amidst the riff-raff from the camp site was too awful to contemplate. The prospect of a clean linen tablecloth and being waited on won the day. And if there were fish on the menu, perhaps some local trout, that would be excellent. Mrs. Burke was leading her up the stairs to a gallery-like landing, towards an open door. With a sinking heart—somehow Amanda had expected it—they were entering the room with the balcony.

The ever-voluble servant ushered her into the room and departed to other regions of the house. Amanda surveyed her lodgings. Whilst the deep-set window certainly did nothing to lighten the room, it was by no means as disconcerting as she had expected—another case of letting her imagination run wild. The walls were tastefully decorated in a red patterned William Morris wallpaper, which, if it did not correspond entirely with Amanda's plain preferences, did at least look respectable and welcoming. The room felt well kept and a scented air wafted in from the open French window, its light muslin curtains shimmering in the gentle breeze. The *en suite* facilities (she would not have contemplated otherwise) were adequate, and she was relieved to find a bath rather than a shower. A shower, she always thought, never left one feeling really *clean*; and since she had been ill cleanliness, to Amanda, preceded Godliness as a necessary amulet against the darker side of life. Indeed, a long hot soak in a foaming bath was one of the few pleasures left.

A furtive shifting movement in a far corner of the room startled her, but it was only her reflection in an old free-standing full-length mirror. Amanda regarded herself in the looking-glass, thinking of Alice, wondering if she stepped through to the other side might she then reverse her world of depression for one of joy. But, knowing her luck, she would doubtless meet some fearful Jabberwock or a mad queen imploring her to think of God knows how many impossible things before breakfast. Even as a child she had never been one to contemplate her image with any sense of vanity; and lately the terrible idea always crossed her mind that despite her forty-two years, the face which stared out at her more closely resembled how she would look at seventy-two than she had looked at twenty-two. To distract her miserable thoughts she undressed immediately in preparation for the purging redemption of a bath, delighted at the speed and profusion of the steaming water as it filled the tub. She settled down at last into the water at a temperature just a few degrees short of scalding. As she yielded herself to the blissful depths two small irritating thoughts pestered: she had not yet ventured out onto the balcony, and who was it she thought she had seen there from the train?

Refreshed and rejuvenated, Amanda stood at the balustrade and surveyed the scene. The balcony commanded a surprisingly distant view. Across the laurel hedge and the lane a tumbling kaleidoscope of colour drew the eye naturally down to a gap in a glade of conifers beyond which stretched a wide green meadow, and farther back the rocky pinnacles of Muncaster Fell. She must have been looking straight back to the point on the railway line, skirting its foot, from where she had first glimpsed The Ferns. Just a couple of hours ago, and already it seemed like a lifetime. A movement in the field, maybe a quarter of a mile away, caught her eye. It was a scarecrow flapping in the breeze. It almost looked as if it were waving at her. She had often wondered whether such things did any good, whether the instinct of birds, which after all made their way to Africa and back with no visible means of navigation, could be fooled into mistaking a few flapping rags on a pole for a human being. Another countryside superstition, she thought intolerantly, and no doubt there would be a lot more of those this weekend.

Mrs. Burke had recommended a shortcut to the inn along the green lanes, avoiding the need to take the road, but the confusing series of alternatives persuaded her to press on uphill to the clustered buildings of the village. Large houses flanked the lane; all looked vacant. Amanda consciously acknowledged for the first time how deserted everywhere felt. Indeed, since departing the station she had encountered no sign of humanity other than Mrs. Burke and Mrs. Cardownie, apart from the strains heard from the balcony of yet another crying infant. Perhaps the villagers, like her hostess, were busy getting ready for Beltane.

Rounding a bend, Amanda found herself confronted by a group of oddly dressed figures spreadeagled across the lane; it took some seconds to realise what it was she was seeing. Her heart was palpitating, but it was only a group of gaily-dressed straw figures. They were doubtless connected with the celebrations—effigies, maybe, to set aflame on the moorland bonfires. In the gathering twilight they looked sinister. A drive with a sign led off the road: St. Bethany's School. The figures must be a creation of the children, specially done for the May events.

A few hundred yards and Amanda reached the village green, a blossom-wreathed Old English Maypole sprouted in the middle. On the opposite side of the green she could see the sign: "The Green Man". Its extensive buildings were set amidst a wooded garden. But disappointment awaited. It was too late to get a table in the dining room; she would have to make do with a bar meal. The apologetic young waiter explained there was a large wedding party in that night, but tomorrow she could certainly dine there. Would she like to book a table now? Or was she wanting to partake later of the roast ox on the village green? The inn was organising that. It would be ready about midnight. Just as she thought: drunks stuffing themselves with a barbecue in the middle of the night. She acceded with alacrity to the offer of a booked table for the following evening, stipulating seven-thirty prompt and next to a window.

The bar, like all bars Amanda had ever known, was smoky and stuffy. A group of local men were slumped on stools before the beer pumps or standing with pint glasses in their hands, polluting the air with cigar, cigarette or pipe. It ought to be banned in public. Heads turned in idle curiosity as she made her way to the most remote corner of the murky saloon, selecting a cramped table that at least had the virtue of being by an open door to the garden. There was a burst of ribald laughter, which she knew must be aimed at her from the ostentatious way each man pretended not to look in her direction. Unfortunately there was also a noisy group outside consisting of several youngish women and a gaggle of ill-behaved children. One of them was breastfeeding a baby—*in public*. The children were guzzling away greedily; all were pale and obese. Amanda thought uncharitably of a litter of pigs foraging in a sty. Two youngsters catching sight of her scuttled over, crisp packets in their hands, and stared rudely. The way they were brought up these days! No manners!

Amanda was the only one dining, and was soon being served by the deferential waiter with grilled rainbow trout and salad, washed down with a glass of a somewhat acidic white wine. At least the trout was good, though the salad was limp and uninviting. She ate quickly, still peeved at the closure of the dining room and anxious to escape this den of iniquity. Half-inebriated voices at the bar were loudly and lewdly discussing the forthcoming festivities.

A rugged farmer, attired in filthy blue check shirt, with a face that looked carved from the mountain granite, was regaling his younger companions in a strong gruff accent with some yarn about the old days.

"I tell yer, lads, my grandmother could tell a rit tale 'bout them fires an' goin's on up on moor in them days, an' the goin's on after, dancin' round that Maypole, like! Aye! An' more! You youngsters don't know nowt."

"Didn't they used t'burn virgins on them fires, then?" asked a grinning youth, whose baseball cap seemed tailor-made to enhance his expression of imbecility.

"Aye! An' that wasn't all they did to'em, ha!" growled the farmer. "But reckon all them practices 'ave died out these days!"

"Bloody well have to round here," declared a middle-aged man with an earring and a head shaven to hide his baldness, "None of 'em left! Ha! Ha!"

"An endangered species," shouted the young man, proud of his witticism.

Sympathetic guffaws echoed round the bar. Amanda fumed. Men! Typical! Incapable of holding a conversation without bringing it round to vulgarity and sex. Finishing her unpleasant stewed coffee, she paid the hovering waiter and stepped into the freshness of the night. The explosion of laughter reverberating round the bar as she left was, surely, she felt, at her expense.

The evening was still quite bright as she traversed the village green. A full moon was riding high in the sky, etching in silhouette the sharp contours of the fells and making strange shadows in the trees. Her decision to try and find Mrs. Burke's shortcut in reverse, she told herself, was simply because she wished to enjoy a moonlit walk and nothing to do with a reluctance to run the gauntlet of those weird scarecrows in the road. But locating the path in reverse proved even more difficult than finding its beginning. Amanda was forced willy-nilly back to the road.

But she need not have worried. Evidently the children had removed the effigies for the night. In fact, she just caught a glimpse of one in the pale light, its head bobbing along above the hedge by the drive, propelled by its unseen juvenile chaperone. It was almost as if it were walking. Amanda hurried on, shivering, anxious for a comfortable bed where at last she could rest her travel-weary limbs and submit her agitated mind to that "chief nourisher in life's feast"; the absolution of a deep, untroubled sleep.

Whether it was because she was overtired, had eaten too much or was just unsettled in a strange place, sleep resolutely refused to arrive. The more Amanda tried to force herself to sleep the more awake she became, and she seemed to toss and turn for hours on end. In desperation she put on the bedside light, surprised to find that only forty-five minutes had elapsed. It was a pity she hadn't kept some of the sleeping pills she'd been prescribed, but she'd thrown them all away, disillusioned at the panoply of magic potions offered by the witch-doctors in their vain attempts to roll back the powers of darkness. The best she could do was to try and read.

Amanda had brought only one book with her: Jane Austen's *Emma*, a novel she had read at least once a year since her teens. Emma's romantic machinations would surely settle her. But to her great vexation she could not find the slim volume, though she searched both bags and room. The fact of losing it, of disorder in the universe, bothered her more than not being able to read the book; and it was of sentimental value too, being the very copy she had kept since a girl, worn and battered as it was. Maybe it had fallen from her bag when she was being lectured by Mrs. Burke in the lounge.

Descending the stairs, The Ferns was as silent as the tomb. Amanda sensed that she was all alone in the house. Mrs. Burke probably lived out, but quite where her elusive hostess resided remained a mystery; no sign of Mrs. Cardownie had she seen since her abrupt encounter on arrival. Nor had she solved the puzzle of who it was she had seen from the train standing on the balcony. There was, alas, no sign of *Emma* either. She hoped she hadn't left the book on one of the many trains she'd travelled on that day; absentmindedness had certainly become a problem lately, though she had hoped that giving up the tranquillisers would have helped. Defeated and depressed, with sleep now even more remote, she perused the shelf of "buks", as Mrs. Burke had put it. There was little to entice. *The Shell Guide to Britain.* An excessively technical manual on the birds of Britain. A clutch of well-worn trashy paperbacks. An illustrated biography of Elizabeth I. A motley collection of *Reader's Digest* omnibus editions of abridged novels—and not a title by Jane Austen. There were several Ordnance Survey maps of the area, a few coffee table books on the Lake District, and amongst them an old dull volume that she picked up and opened: written by one Edwina Hale and dated 1951 (a first edition), profusely illustrated with line-drawings and photographs by the author. It was entitled: *Folk and Folklore of Western Cumberland: from Solway to Duddon.*

Most of the major valleys of the west were listed as chapter headings; there was one on Eskdale. Amanda scanned the black and white photographs, of which there were many, and found one of an old sixteenth century print showing villagers dancing round a Maypole. It was the Green. The

Green Man was recognisable in the background, much the same as it looked now. Following the page reference she located the relevant section and began to read. It was remarkable (or perhaps not) how closely the account dovetailed with Mrs. Burke's recent monologue. Under a section entitled, "The Beltane Fires", she read:

Those familiar with Sir James Frazer's famous study of magic and religion, *The Golden Bough*, may recall his account (pp. 617-622, abridged edition, 1922) of the infamous Beltane Fires that appear to be survivals of Celtic practices in Scotland, variously associated with fertility rites and rituals to ward off sorcery. Therein he writes: "In the Central Highlands of Scotland, bonfires, known as the Beltane Fires, were formerly kindled with great ceremony on the first of May, and the traces of human sacrifice at them were particularly clear and unequivocal. The custom of lighting the bonfires lasted in various places far into the eighteenth century, and the descriptions of the ceremony by writers of that period present such a curious and interesting picture of ancient heathendom surviving in our own country that I will reproduce them in the words of their authors. The fullest of the descriptions is the one bequeathed to us by John Ramsay, laird of Ochtertyre, near Crieff, the patron of Burns and the friend of Sir Walter Scott. He says: 'But the most considerable of the Druidical festivals is that of Beltane, or Mayday, which was lately observed in some parts of the Highlands with extraordinary ceremonies . . . Like the other public worship of the Druids, the Beltane feast seems to have been performed on hills or eminences.

They thought it degrading to him whose temple is the universe, to suppose that he would dwell in any house made with hands. The sacrifices were therefore offered in the open air, frequently upon the tops of hills, where they were presented with the grandest views of nature, and were nearest the seat of warmth and order.' "

Although Frazer cites the spread of similar practices to places as diverse as Wales, Ireland and parts of Europe, he makes no reference to Cumberland. It is herein that I offer the product of my own humble researches into local custom and superstition. Despite the depredations of the Vikings, pockets of Celtic survival can still be found in the region extending from the Solway down as far as Barrow-in-Furness, bearing witness to southern migrations from across the Firth in Dumfries and Galloway and no doubt from beyond the Clyde and the Highlands and Islands. In Western Cumberland to this day ceremonies take place each year on the first Sunday in May. Fires are still lit on the Great Moor, where stand the remains of five very ancient stone circles. The Moor, unremarkable in itself and but a mile from the village of Greendale, commands a sublime position in relation to the higher eminences around. To stand here alone with the grass gently rustling in the wind on a fair Spring day and the larks chattering invisibly up above is indeed to feel oneself close to "the seat of warmth and order" and to behold "the grandest views of nature." Local lore has it that the fires, which are attended after feasting on a freshly slaughtered ox and following a Maypole dance on the village green, replicate the superstitious pagan rites in which not two hundred years ago "a maiden pure and true" was still consigned to the flames to propitiate the nature spirits and protect the newborn of the Spring. It would seem, here, that the purpose had evolved from Scottish practices where the emphasis was traditionally upon the protection of the year's crops. It is thought that exceptionally high infant mortality rates during the Dark Ages, possibly connected with Norse "massacres of the innocents" may have wrought this local change. In this modern era carnival effigies are committed to the bonfires, and the whole occasion is in the manner of a rustic Guy Fawkes Night. It is a gay and joyous event in which the children play a prominent role. No traveller to Cumberland should miss this festival be they here in the fair month of May when the blossoms and the scents are here unsurpassed.

Strange, thought Amanda, how coincidences arise: that she should have stumbled on this account by such fortuitous circumstances on the very eve of the festivities themselves. That explained the effigies, and they were in the charge of the children; she had been right in her guesswork. The moor, at least, sounded fascinating and well worth a visit. She would have been tempted to go there tomorrow had she not already planned to take the steam train to Ravenglass and make her way back with a good hike along the top of Muncaster Fell. Yawning, sleepy at last, she climbed the stairs, almost stumbling over the cat, invisible in the darkness of the hall. She sank into the luxury of the double bed and collapsed exhausted into slumber.

But, as often happens when sleep is caught too late, Amanda slept fitfully, waking suddenly in a panic at first light, heart racing, with the remnants of a shocking nightmare stalking her consciousness. She could hear the birds starting to sing. She sat up and turned on the bedside light, trying to recall the dream, to piece together the fragments of the horror. If she dozed off again, it might continue . . . In the dream she had been young again . . . revelling in the litheness of her limbs, the freshness of her skin, the unutterable peacefulness of her mind . . . but then by the arcane logic of a nightmare this carefree sense, this joy, this sheer optimism at existence, transmuted into a nameless fear, an all-pervading dread, the worst abysses of a nervous breakdown with something worse, imminent and ill-defined . . .

She was being driven by ugly porcine children up the lane from The Ferns, taunted and punched by tiny malevolent fists until, like Christ arriving at Calvary, she reached the village green. The air was wreathed with the choking smell of wood smoke, mingling with untold miasmic blossom scents, and there was a yowling of babes. The men from the pub were around, grinning. It was like a scene from Breughel or Bosch. To her shame and horror she suddenly became aware that she was naked. Above her loomed a tall, branchless silver birch, serving as a Maypole. Its crown was lost in a smoky haze. Small, eager hands were lashing her to the trunk, laughing in preparation for the final humiliation . . .

What was so repulsive about the dream was the way she had been able to imagine in such intimate detail acts of which she had no direct experience.

Indeed, so unclean was the memory, Amanda decided to take another bath and dress in the fresh new hiking clothes she had bought (at not inconsiderable expense) especially for the trip. Then she would set out for a long purifying tramp on the hills.

Soon she was sitting with a good strong morning cup of tea in a reclining wicker chair on the balcony. The eastern sun, though obscured from her position, illuminated the distant slopes of the fell, painting the landscape before her into a scene by Monet. It was a pure, pure morning, banishing the nightmare to a foolish insubstantiality. Reading about those ridiculous local customs just before going to sleep had done it. Except for the glorious cacophony of the birds' dawn chorus, and the faint whining of a baby from a neighbouring villa, the world was silent. Beautiful and silent. An unreal feeling of calm, even bliss, seeped into Amanda as she sipped the first stimulating mouthfuls of tea. She hadn't felt like this in years. Maybe she was getting better after all?

Some two hours were wanting before the first train of the day would pass through, on its way back to the coast. Amanda decided to while away the time with an early morning wander round the village. Mrs. Burke had left in the dining room for her—the room across the hall from the lounge—a continental breakfast, if such a phrase could be used to describe the arid white rolls and marmalade set out on a table by the window. There was also a packed lunch of an orange, an apple, a cheese sandwich, and fruitcake, which she neatly arranged along with local maps and *Emma* (it had been there all the time!) in her rucksack. There was no sign of Mrs. Burke or Mrs. Cardownie, only the cat, preening itself with an air of Olympian detachment in a sunny spot on the rug, until, suddenly alert, it seemed to stare right through her.

Amanda stepped out into the cool freshness of the morning, curiously alive despite her poor night's sleep, and roamed in desultory fashion along the labyrinthine lanes in continued amazement at how uplifted she felt, even euphoric. Yet in the background was the apprehension that her mood could change as unpredictably to its opposite; oh yes, there had been many false dawns. This time, however, in a way she could not quite describe, it felt somehow different: a sense almost of exultation, or possibly even exaltation.

Several of the gates she passed bore signs: "Garden Open Today"—no doubt connected with the weekend celebrations. One she entered. It climbed steeply up a rocky hillside. A phalanx of azaleas and nameless flowering shrubs soared before her. The path led Amanda, serpentinely, up through a series of seemingly endless secret gardens. The colours and the smells were fantastic; it was like stumbling through the back door into Paradise. From a craggy promontory she surveyed her surroundings, now so familiar, yet so strange. She could see the railway line, where it left the confines of the houses and crossed a buttercup-embroidered meadow towards the flanks of the fell, alongside which it would be transporting her in an hour or so.

Amanda was suddenly overcome by the conviction that she did not want to leave, even for an afternoon; that the little toy train would merely carry her back to a cold reality, to depression, to the dark cave of her previous life. A voice in her head was reprimanding her, telling her that she must stick to her original plan. But the time had come for change. Another part of her, like the burgeoning blooms all around her, was awakening to a new morning. Already she was thinking of "the grandest views of nature" from the Great Moor.

Scarcely more than twelve hours had elapsed since her arrival in the village and already she was enveloped in its magic. The grim white walls of the psychiatric ward and its myriad lost souls, the mumbo-jumbo of the witch-doctors, the cold constriction of the world, all crumbled behind, detritus of a hollow life. As Amanda gazed into the glittering mystery of the landscape it was like a revelation, like the strange sad harmonies of an old Scottish ballad, echoing on the brink of an almost-grasped, yet ultimately unattainable truth. She must have been gazing longer than she had realised, for she could hear the sound of the steam engine puffing and tooting its whistle as it drew into the halt, lost somewhere in the shimmering glades below. As she watched it emerge from the trees and depart towards the coast, it was as if she were witnessing the last lifeline to her past disappearing in the silent distance.

Now, with the entire day before her to explore the moor, Amanda felt a welcome sense of liberation. In her present mood of gaiety she thought she would first investigate the activities in the village as its denizens prepared for the night's festivities. And there would be a chance to look more closely at the scarecrows before they were immolated on the hillside. Rounding the bend in the bright morning light, they no longer looked so terrifying, especially as she now knew both their provenance and their fate. The children must have been up very early because already the effigies were distributed around the entrance to the school and even at strategic points on the road, secured safely in place to trees, road signs and railings. One, dressed in an ancient brown checked suit, spectacles and battered trilby, was sitting on an old bench. They faced every direction with their outstretched arms and inane smiles. Yet for all their patent artificiality there was something horribly lifelike about them, their very essence as a parody investing them with an air of indefinable menace.

Amanda faced each one in turn, deconstructing them with ridicule—products of children's fantasy. The one on the bench, who was wearing odd socks, she called the professor. Two males, clad in torn, washed-out denim, tied to a speed-limit sign, looked not unlike her obnoxious nephews. Two females, on either side of a sycamore trunk, sported flowing golden locks, fashioned from torn-up raffia matting. The taller wore a blue and white sailor top and a brightly coloured patchwork skirt. The other, decidedly scruffy, wore a loose green velvet dress. The latter, she christened Arabella, and her more elegant sister, Esmeralda. Esmeralda vaguely reminded her of someone, or something long ago, a dim and dreamlike memory. Her thoughts were interrupted.

"Will you be coming to our fair? We open around ten." A woman of about her own age, with a healthy outdoor complexion, was addressing her, smiling warmly. "Fine morning, isn't it?" She was well-spoken but with the recognisable local lilt. "We're hoping it stays fine for the fires tonight. Are you staying locally?" She was leading a surly child by the hand, who fixed his narrow eyes on Amanda with suspicion.

Without waiting for a reply, she continued, "We hold it every year—arts and crafts—here in the school." She was pointing up the drive beyond the scarecrows. Catching Amanda's glance, she gesticulated round the grinning effigies. "D'you like them? The children made them. I'm Roberta, by the way . . . We'll see you in a while then?"

Her final words, Amanda thought, had been delivered more in a tone of assumption than invitation, and she decided she must be one of the teachers; her voice alone, pitched several decibels above the norm, confirmed this. Still, she had been well-meaning, and Amanda decided to come back after she'd bought some sparkling water at the village stores to drink with her lunch; she would still have the most of the day for her journey to the hills. Maybe she might buy something at the fair, a memento of what was promising to be her first happy day in months.

But it proved not to have been a wise idea. The school room was very crowded. The teachers were conversing in foghorn voices and the many children were unruly. Most resembled the obese louts she had encountered in the bar, and there were vulgar, noisy teenagers. Numerous young mothers and grandmothers were nursing babies; by the sound of their whinging the infants were as irked at the proceedings as Amanda. Roberta floated round, evincing no sign of interest or even recognition. The crafts for sale proved as unremarkable as they were overpriced, while the offerings by local artists were clearly the product of enthusiasm rather than talent. But there were two that caught her eye.

One, not too badly executed, portrayed a wild upland moor surrounded by menacing hills with remnants of standing stones dominating the foreground. It was entitled, simply, *The Great Moor*. The other, which could charitably only be described as an amateur's tribute to the Pre-Raphaelites, gave her a bit of a turn: it was unmistakably a picture of The Ferns. A young girl with flowing tresses of fair hair stood leaning at the balustrade, like Juliet awaiting Romeo. It was entitled *The Damsel in Distress*. The figure's posture struck some hidden chord in Amanda's mind, a vague resemblance perhaps to somebody, but so cartoon-like was the execution that she decided in the end that the resemblance was to none other than raffia-haired Esmeralda. The fair was proving all a bit disturbing, a wrong note in the harmony of this so far too perfect day, and Amanda wished she could escape immediately to the vastness of the moor. But at least the strong brown liquid, served in delicate china cups from a great urn by a pleasant old lady with white pageboy hair, was authentic, reassuring Women's Institute tea.

Amanda traced the circuitous route of ascent quite easily; it was as if she knew the way already, or the great green moor was guiding her with a will and purpose of its own.

The ecstasy that had gripped her earlier that day, clouded briefly by the fair, was now replenished. But how long, she wondered, could it really last? The sun was hot, a lovely cooling breeze blowing off the sea. She felt fit and agile, as she had not known in many years. A bluebell-strewn oak wood, a wooden stile across a mossy wall, then suddenly she was there on the open fell, freedom all around. A wide, undulating, grassy upland, with stands of flaming broom and gorse, spanned the horizon. When she found the summit she would have her lunch.

Locating the top, however, proved unexpectedly prolonged, for the moor was complex and deceptive. There was no sign of the huge pyres she had assumed would be awaiting the celebrations, nor anything resembling Stonehenge. Ascending further, however, it became apparent she was only on a lower slope. Maybe half a mile away she could discern a higher plateau on which stood a single tall stone, pointing to the heavens like a long, thin finger. As she drew near, breathless from the steady climb, she could see scattered boulders, which proved on close inspection to be the remains of stone circles. She counted five in a wide circumference around the broad expanse of the summit. They were rather disappointing, many of the original stones no doubt pillaged long ago for the intake walls. The pyres too were unimpressive, mostly small clumps of twigs and branches. Only one, close to the big stone, looked like a serious effort at a bonfire. Surprisingly, on this very day of the festivities there was not a soul in sight, nor indeed had she passed anyone on the way. Amanda had the immensity of the moor to herself.

Standing by the looming monolith Amanda regarded the encircling panorama. The situation was impressive; even as Edwina Hale had described it, truly a place of the Gods. The ancients had chosen their temple well.

The comparatively modest elevation—maybe a thousand feet—seemed to have been selected with mathematical precision, to maximise the grandeur of the surrounding scene. The high peaks around the valley head were like a too-romantic nineteenth century etching. West, floating on a sunlit sea, the Isle of Man looked strangely near. Most dramatic was the aspect of the southern fells. The view now beheld by Amanda resembled an old Chinese landscape with fantastic mountain shapes rimmed one behind another. Yoadcastle was a frowning giant, Stainton Pike an alpine horn, whilst beyond in serried ranks soared Hesk, Whitfell and the crenellated fortress of Buckbarrow, and finally the arching whale-back of Black Combe. It was a holy—or perhaps, rather, an unholy—place.

Amanda shivered, ruminating on the countless sacrifices offered over untold years at this terrible shrine to the Ancient Gods. The sun had retreated into cloud, an unfriendly wind was blowing up, rustling the pale grass across the fellside, and far away was a boom of thunder. The moor now looked inhospitable, and she felt her spirits fall like a barometer. Her depression persisted even when the sun briefly returned, brightening her picnic. As she ate, Amanda pondered the strangeness of her moods that day. Was her earlier euphoria a symptom of recovery—or something worse? There were forms of schizophrenia, she knew, marked by volatile emotional swings. Hebephrenics cry at joys and laugh on being told bad news. But when she'd be afraid to go outside her flat and thought she was suffering from catatonia, Dr. Quayle had assured her it was just neurosis, only nerves. Whatever way she looked at it, Amanda thought, she was bound to lose. In a sombre frame of mind she took her leave of the summit, descending rapidly to Greendale.

The village was deserted, all activity at the school finished. The scarecrows were still there, though Amanda had an idea some had changed positions, and she now counted nine when previously she thought there were eight. She could not for the life of her conclude which was the newcomer. Esmeralda grinned at her as she passed, guarding some enigmatic secret, her raffia hair moving in the windy flurries. Her outstretched arms made Amanda think uneasily of a crucifixion. She wondered how on earth she had found anything amusing about them that morning; they really were quite grotesque. Yes, the best thing was to cremate them all. She heard the church clock chiming seven, later than expected; she must have lingered longer on the moor than she'd thought—though already Amanda had noticed how unreal time had become in this place. And there was little time to waste if she were to make it to her lonely table at the inn for dinner.

Back at The Ferns all was deserted too, apart from the cat, scrutinising her with a languid air from the porch steps. It tensed at her approach, then as swiftly twisted its head and furiously licked the fur around its shoulder. Of Mrs. Cardownie or Mrs. Burke there was neither sight nor sound. Even the old servant's unceasing prattle would have been preferable to the sultry silence of the house. Dust motes danced in strange swirling patterns as Amanda traversed the empty hall in the shafts of evening sunlight, filtering through the stained glass. She felt exhausted, utterly worn out by the unaccustomed exercise that day and the rollercoaster of her emotions.

Standing at last in the cool shade of the balcony, the world beyond was silent too. Resting wearily upon the balustrade Amanda suddenly recalled *The Damsel in Distress*. She was standing in the same posture, and it struck her with disquieting force just who the damsel reminded her of. It was not so much grim, gay, ragged

Esmeralda—though there was an uncanny likeness—but her own self, captured many years ago in her teens, in a photograph, leaning on the railing of a hotel balcony on the promenade at Southport . . . She was on holiday with Mum and Dad . . . She could even remember the new clothes she was wearing, displaying them happily to her parents—a blue and white sailor top and a brightly coloured patchwork skirt . . .

Silently Amanda wept as she turned her face towards the remnants of the sunlight, longing for the purity and tranquillity of those days. If there were any consolation it was the knowledge that it would all soon be over. She thought with a vague and distant regret of the empty candlelit table, the crisp clean linen, the shining silver cutlery awaiting her at The Green Man, and sighed.

She stared out wistfully across the rambling coloured gardens, glorious and perfect as Poe's "Domain of Arnheim", out through the gap in the conifers and beyond towards the fell, the yellow broom and gorse blazing in the dying rays of the sunset. Why was it, Amanda reflected, that behind all beauty lay a knife of pain? She could hear the strains of music getting nearer all the time, a slowly beating drum, melancholy pipes, the delicate strumming of a lute. There was a sad tune floating down the air, mingling with the scents and shades of the glorious blooms like a mystic revelation. It was an old Scottish ballad:

Oh! The Broom, the Bonny, Bonny, Broom.

It was a sure symptom of madness, she knew, to confuse scent, sound and colour; in the trade they called it synaesthesia, but to Amanda it came as deliverance.

The celebrants were advancing at a solemn pace along the lane from the village, up towards The Ferns. At the front marched white-robed Mrs. Cardownie, tailed by a straggling band of animal-guised revellers and a column of laughing children. Then came Mrs. Burke. The musicians followed, draped like medieval minstrels, and after them the young mothers, holding up their whining newborn babes. And at the rear stalked Esmeralda and her grotesque companions, shambling along in a hideous parody of human locomotion. A smell of newly kindled fire came wafting down from the skies. When the procession stormed the garden Amanda was quite unable to decide whether the balustrade offered confinement or protection. But did she really care anymore?

There was a crashing in the hallway and a stumping up the staircase. The door into her room burst open wide. A figure shifted across the floor. Through the thin muslin curtains of the balcony a raffia-matted face was grinning into hers, like her reflection in a crazy mirror. Arms of straw reached out from a blue and white sailor top . . . it was almost a caress . . .

Born aloft, up the twisting path to the moor, Amanda wondered why what she was feeling was not so much terror as elation.

M. E. F.

Record of a Visit to Iona, November 1999

Thursday, November 11th
10.00 PM

I have arrived at last on Iona's fair shores. I did not think I would ever get here. The weather has been atrocious for days. The passage across the Sound of Iona from Fionnphort is a mere ten minutes. This evening it took forty. Even the crossing from Oban, on a larger vessel, was badly delayed, but they held the connecting bus, and the Iona ferry. They would not do that these days on the railways! This is not the first time I have been to Iona, but it is the first time I have actually come to stay on the island. The first time I came was in June, five years since, and I was with Alida.

Rain lashes at the windows and the gales roar, but the Argyll Hotel is welcoming. Log fires blaze in the lounges. It is delightfully old-fashioned. There are no televisions— what a haven! I only wish Alida were with me; she would have enjoyed it here. I am very tired. I think I shall sleep despite the demons in my mind. They say that Iona brings healing—though I fear I am beyond that.

M. E. F.

I did not sleep well at all. The storm strengthened in the night. It sounded as if the roof was being torn off; it is made of corrugated iron, which apparently is more durable than slates up here, but it makes an unholy rattling. And the wind! I have never heard anything like it! It was as if an anguished voice were crying outside my window. It distressed me and spun mournful dreams.

The storm subsided at dawn. Before breakfast I walked as far as the abbey. The day is fresh and invigorating, a scent in the air of something indefinable, evoking associations that remain just out of reach. I watched the sun breaking through the clouds over Mull, wreathed around Ben More. The pinkish-red stone of the abbey glowed like flame in the rising sun. I can see why Columba chose here to found Christianity. The *light* is so vivid, giving colours a surreal intensity. I visited the Reilig Odhráin, resting place of the ancient kings of Scotland, and found the grave. On the north side of St. Oran's Chapel, two low stones mark its extent; and a tiny open book, made of marble, embedded in the green turf, with its terse inscription: *M.E.F. Aged 33 Years. Died 19 November 1929.* Such economy of words, so tragic the tale! A tale of one who heard Iona's call.

We first came upon the grave, Alida and I, in the course of an exploration of the antiquarian sites of the West. It is now almost three years since Alida passed away, not so far from here, out there to the north, on another island, at the edge of the vast Atlantic. It feels longer, and yet in some ways only yesterday. Time ceases to have much meaning for me, if indeed it has any meaning at all. There is a peril in the Hebrides, for those who heed their melody—the Ballad of Grey Weather (as John Buchan calls it), making

33

those who hear it sick all the days of their life for something they cannot name. I come to these shores in tribute to Alida—and in the footsteps of M.E.F.

An icy wind blows despite the brightness. The Black Wind of the North, they call it here. It etches the far hills and isles in stark, charcoal silhouette and keeps the murky south-westerlies at bay. Only one other person was abroad this chilly morn, a hardy Scottish lass draped in the fringed Hebridean shawl.

9.30 PM

I spent today re-familiarising myself with the island— the immediate vicinity at least—trying to absorb its atmosphere. It is so peaceful without the summer sightseers, the day trip pilgrims. I spent some time in the ruins of the Augustinian nunnery, and visited the well of eternal youth on the hill of Dùn Ì. More adventurous plans can wait; I have several days here. During the afternoon the wind swung round to the east. It got no warmer. There is a hint of drizzle in the air and the forecast is bad.

The Argyll Hotel is indeed exquisite. Oak panelling, parquet floors, antiques. A delightfully dilapidated conservatory overlooks the sound, where I took afternoon tea. The guests are few: three lone elderly ladies, immersed in books, refugees like myself to this sanctuary of peace; also two African nuns, who beam beatifically; and a stern-faced clergyman—they have business at the abbey; and two middle-aged Irish women, who whisper animatedly about things New Age. Our young waitresses are cheerful and capable. They are not Scottish—there was some language misunderstanding at breakfast as to how I liked my eggs. I would guess from their accents they are Eastern European. The stylish girl who ushered me into the restaurant this evening, however, speaks better English, though she sounds foreign too; quite elegant, with long tresses of black hair tied in plaits. She looks more Latin than Slav. I rather like her. Her name is Mhairi (pronounced Var-ee), a Celtic name, so perhaps she *is* Scottish after all; there is Hispanic blood in the Hebrides dating back to galleons wrecked during the Spanish Armada. Indeed, on Barra and Eriskay they look positively swarthy.

It is still a trial for me to holiday alone in Scotland. I miss Alida—with a deep, consuming passion. I return each November, to be here on her anniversary.

Saturday, November 13th
11.00 AM

The forecast was right. Today is abominable in a way only Scottish weather can be. A grim, grey canopy of cloud overhangs the island, and the rain is of that fine, persistent, drenching sort which renders any kind of outdoor exploration as pointless as it is unpleasant. The only thing to do is stay indoors and hope conditions improve. The fires are already lit and inviting. I may even get a chance to chat more with Mhairi. I saw her again this morning, outside in the rain, when I walked up to St. Oran's. She smiled, I think, in recognition. She holds a strange attraction for me, perhaps because she reminds me a little of Alida when she was young. But I must guard against such foolish infatuations.

I forgot to mention the hotel's finest asset: its enormous collection of old books. Everywhere, on staircases, landings, along corridors, shelves of them. It is like staying in a library. Many are dry as dust, but there are gems too. There is much Scottish topography, natural history and folklore. I noted books by Fiona Macleod, Herbert J.

Boyd's *Strange Tales of the Western Isles*, and numerous titles by Seton Gordon and Alasdair Alpin MacGregor. When I asked last night where they all came from, Mhairi merely smiled, bemused—as if anyone would ask such a question! It bothers me Mhairi might think me odd. I have already formed the impression that the other waitresses do.

6.00 PM

The rain has persisted all day. (As one of the Irish ladies aptly put it to me, "It hasn't stopped since it started.") I have passed an idle afternoon amidst the hotel's books. I looked for books on Iona that might shed further light on M.E.F. But those I found proved either to have been printed before 1929, or not to mention her at all. My interest in her tragedy arose originally from a casual antiquarianism (in which Alida shared); but, reading about it in the dark months following Alida's own sad death, I realise I have developed an obsessive fascination, which I cannot fully explain or understand, except to say that the parallel tragedies seem to weave within my mind a tapestry of intertwining grief. There is a view that grief, once time has done its healing, should be left behind, but for some grief remains a permanent, necessary indulgence, the only way the dead can be kept alive; and if this is superstition, what else in this extraordinary world is not? I fear I spend too much time alone since Alida died. Morbid thoughts besiege me.

9.00 PM

I am certainly right about the staff thinking me odd. Mhairi must have been off duty tonight and I was served again by the girl who got the eggs wrong. Her name is

Ilsa. I fear I must take back my assertion that the staff are capable; and this time language can't be blamed! I sat for an unconscionable time at my table. When Ilsa eventually came over, she looked perplexed and asked me if I wished to order now. On pointing out that I had been sitting there for twenty minutes, she said, "I thought you were waiting for the lady", or words to that effect. Only then did I notice that the table had been set for two. Of course, I do have a double room and the table numbers match the rooms, but it's not the first time she has served me. Amidst profuse apologies she spirited away the surplus cutlery and crockery and brought the soup. But then I saw her with another waitress, looking over in my direction, smirking. The incident dispirited me, bringing home how lonely my travels have become since Alida. She would have made great jest of the error—and the eggs. How I miss the trills of Alida's laughter, her stirring company. And the weather doesn't help. If anything, it gets worse. Maybe it will blow itself out by morning.

Sunday, November 14th
9.00 AM

A better day is in prospect. Already the skies are clearing. I am glad, for today is Alida's anniversary. It is also Sunday and for the first time in my life I shall attend Holy Communion, though I am not a practising Christian. Perhaps I want to merge into Iona's spiritual aura, to absorb its essence through ritual? How Alida would laugh at such superstition!

I cannot deny that there is a strange *otherness* about Iona. Maybe it is the weight of centuries of sacred pilgrimage? To wander through the ruins of the ancient nunnery, then beside the sea to St. Oran's and the Reilig Odhráin, and the abbey, with its medieval crosses, is to know the isle in all its eerie glory. There are marvellous carvings on the cloister pillars, part of recent restoration; they follow a cycle, beginning and ending at Alpha and Omega, sculptured in the form of a serene face, with flowing hair. Even before Columba, this place was sacred—though Christians might say profane. There is an aspect to its mystical quality that, I must confess, is not entirely comfortable. There is a painting in the north transept, a crucifixion by an unnamed artist, that could make one scream—whether with agony or ecstasy I would not like to say. Last night again my sleep was restless, with only the mournful wind for company; it was as if a voice were keening in sorrow outside my window— or singing in melancholic rhapsody.

8.30 PM

Today has proved, indeed, a day of great rapture! At times I felt as if my grief were being transmuted through Iona's alchemy into bittersweet nostalgia, my sadness into exultation. It began with Holy Communion. The singing was led by a young woman from Bucharest, who took us through a call-and-response intonation of the Kyrie Eleison, which echoed gloriously around the abbey. She read from Thomas Traherne, Swedenborg and an obscure Romanian theologian, as well as the Book of Revelation. Throughout the service sparrows wheeled and chirped high up in the nave, like holy spirits. As I sipped the bitter Communion wine—the Blood of Our Lord Jesus Christ— it was as if my veins were being infused with the Holy Spirit of Iona! The final hymn was "Immortal, Invisible". We were singing the lines "In Light Inaccessible, Hid from our eyes". Low sunbeams were catching the panes of the east window, glinting sapphire, lilac, rose-carmethine.

Tears came to my eyes, a vast immanence engulfed me. For, do not the scientists now teach, even as did Swedenborg and Traherne, the Transcendence of the Light?

In the Chapel of Healing I lit a candle for Alida, and another for M.E.F.

Later I trod the white sands of the northern shore, where Viking ghosts are said to appear. I was solitary except for one distant figure. I lingered as the ocean crashed inexorably; huge, long-rolling breakers. The wind was moving round into the north-west—full circuit of the compass in two days! That's what I love about the Hebrides: the restless, constant change. It resonates with something in my soul—though I know I am not the first. I watched the thin line of Alida's island emerge on the northern horizon in a kind of serendipitous memoriam. I gazed, as once did Kathleen Raine—she who cursed the rowan at Camusfearna—as she looked back, north from Iona's shores, in memory of her friend, Gavin Maxwell, to a place now removed not so much by space as by time: "Leaving you, I have come to Iona's strand, Where the far is near, and the dear, far, Since not again can I be with you life with life, I would be with you as star with distant star, As drop of water in the one bright bitter sea."

11.30 PM

It is a clear, frosty night, almost full moon, the distant peaks of Mull dimly visible. The scent of snow is in the air. The constellations arch above the island, a canopy of iridescence; near enough, it seems, to touch, yet illimitably, vertiginously distant, the Milky Way a dazzling highway to infinity, spectacular, terrifying. I have returned from a stroll as far as St. Oran's (to shake off the sluggishness of the wine and the fire). I am not sure it was a good idea.

I was drawing near the Reilig Odhráin. A bluish radiance was flickering over the cemetery. At first I thought I was suffering an ocular disturbance, but then decided it to be an illusion: a distortion of the light from the "eternal flame" that burns within the dim recesses of St. Oran's Chapel. (This "eternal flame" is a form of candle, and I find it hard to believe it is never extinguished, in the winds they have here; it is probably *symbolically* eternal, constantly reignited; I have never yet seen it out.) For reasons I cannot name, I was filled with a brooding apprehension. Yet, when I recognised what I was seeing, I could have wept for joy. The Northern Lights! Aurora Borealis! To Hebrideans, the Merry Dancers—said to be the angels cast from Heaven when Lucifer rebelled. They flashed and pulsed through infinities of blue, like tongues of fire detaching from the flame of St. Oran's. It was eerie. A crazy idea came upon me that it would be a fine night to be out on the moors, that I should go there forthwith. To watch the moonlight streaming silver on the ocean. The colours scintillating in the northern skies. Truly this was a night to tear aside the veil, a night to behold the angels. But perish such thoughts. They do not feel like my own. Even now, by the blazing fire, I shiver uncontrollably— with cold or exhilaration, I am unsure.

Monday, November 15th
4.00 PM

Today has been another atrocious day. It seemed scarcely conceivable, after last night's clear skies, to awake this morning to swirling rain. I am not feeling well—tired and drained, though I slept deeply. I passed the time productively enough, noting down all I can remember about M.E.F.

M. E. F.

Marie Emily Fornario arrived on Iona in the summer of 1929, thirty-three years of age. Like many, she came to Iona's sacred shores in search of spiritual calm, believing she had lived here in a previous life, that she was called. Intending only to stay a few days, she never left. She became fascinated by the southern moors, that region of the island to this day known as evil, where Pagan forces vie with Christian, and darkness challenges the light. Here she was wont to wander at odd hours of the night, in all weathers, but especially when the moon was bright. One November she went out and did not return. Two days later they found her dead in bizarre circumstances: sprawled on the moor in a peat hollow, hacked out in the shape of a cross with a knife by her corpse, naked but for a black cape. Her feet were bloody from stumbling (or running) through the heather. It is rumoured that where her body was discovered a small cairn was erected. It is my ambition to find that cairn.

Marie Emily Fornario was an aesthete, mingling with the literati of London. She wrote mystical poetry and reviewed esoteric opera, like Rutland Boughton's *The Immortal Hour* (a Celtic allegory of Spring's resurrection, the banishing of Winter). Daughter of an Italian professor and an English mother, deceased since childhood, she lived alone in Mortlake Road, Kew. She had an interest in occult and psychic phenomena; a member of the Alpha and Omega Sect, of the Hermetic Order of the Golden Dawn, amongst whose members numbered William Sharp, who wrote (under the pseudonym Fiona Macleod) studies of Iona's spiritual lore known to have influenced Miss Fornario. (Indeed, these same books inspired Boughton's opera; and I have been reading in bed Sharp's *Iona*). She was an intimate friend of occultist Dion Fortune (aka Violet Firth), author of *The Secrets of*

Dr. Taverner and *Psychic Self-Defence*. A Theosophist, Miss Fornario believed she had been reincarnated, and that in Iona she would witness the Light Transcendent.

In the sober island community Marie Fornario cut an arresting presence: in the dark cape and handwoven garments of the Arts and Crafts Movement, with her long, plaited raven locks, her glittering jewellery, and, it is said, a distant look in her eyes, as if she gazed beyond the forms of this world. Staying with the Camerons, a farming family at Traighmor, overlooking the Sound of Iona, she rapidly won their hearts, for her sensitivity and warmth, and for the interest she displayed in their tales of local folklore. But her increasingly strange behaviour caused her hosts alarm—though never alienation, for all that her activities conflicted with their dour Presbyterianism. For their lodger, never in robust heath, took to sleeping through the day, falling into trances, fasting, and spending long nights out on the moors. She burned tiny oil-lamps in her room throughout the long dark hours, and spoke of visions and voices in the heavens, and journeys to the Far Beyond.

As the grim Hebridean winter closed in, Miss Fornario's state of mind worsened; where once her eccentricity had seemed to bring inner peace, now it was infused with harrowing spiritual terror, with fear and trembling. One day, in great agitation, she declared she must leave the island forthwith; but, it being the Sabbath, no ferry was running, and she was persuaded to await the morn. But by the day's end her mood had changed, and she announced in perfect calm that she would remain on Iona after all. Writing to a London acquaintance, she confided she could not leave Iona because she had "a terrible case of healing on". What that phrase meant remains a mystery. But do I already, here on Iona's sacred shores, begin to understand?

In the early hours, Miss Fornario left Traighmor and was never seen alive again. Her death upon the moors was attributed to exhaustion and exposure, for the nights were bitter and frosty.

Miss Fornario's strange demise was embellished by the local press, variant versions appearing in *The Oban Times*, *The Glasgow Herald* and *The Scotsman*: that jewellery she wore turned black overnight; that the lack of marks on her bare feet suggested levitation; that blue lights flickered where she died and around her grave; that a man in a dark cloak was witnessed; that her father had a premonition; that she was digging in the ground to release fairies; that the kitchen knife found by her body was a ritual dagger; and that her ghost walked abroad upon the moors. The case appeared in *The Occult Review*, gilded by Dion Fortune, who alleged unnatural death, the result of psychic attack, which Miss Fornario had courted by reckless journeys on the Astral Plane; even that she was murdered by the spirit of the sixteen-month-deceased Mina Mathers, founder of Alpha and Omega. Subsequent accounts err still further: she is Norah, or Netta; Fornario is spelt Farnario; her hosts were the MacRaes, not the Camerons; and there is inconsistency as to where she lay, a fallacy being that it was on the weird-sounding Fairy Mound. Not the least of difficulties—if I ever get there in this weather—will be to know even where to begin the search, let alone find the cairn.

Tuesday, November 16th
8.00 AM

Today I *must go to the moors*. The day promises to brighten, so there is no excuse.

6.00 PM

My search of the moors has been, regrettably, frustrating. I took the Pilgrims' Path, climbing up by the Staonaig Lochan. The moorland is confusing, with endless undulations, rocky outcrops, hollows and steep corries plunging to the sea; a three-dimensional labyrinth. It has a vastness and complexity out of all proportion to its size, which can scarcely exceed a square mile. It was like looking for a needle in a haystack. A problem is that no account offers specific indication as to where her corpse was found (except, spuriously, to the Fairy Mound). It is more reliably said she was heading for the ancient ruins of Dun Lathraichean, a site of spectral fascination. In the nineteenth century two terrified nuns claimed to have witnessed on the hill an inexplicable conflagration. Miss Fornario claimed that here she heard the voices of the angels and saw visions in the skies.

I had little wish to linger on the Dun, which I found, indeed, an uneasy place, and proceeded to the Carn Cul ri Eirinn. (The Cairn Looking Back to Ireland, so-called because Iona was the first place Columba came where he could *not* see Ireland.) The promontory on which it stands overlooks the ocean, with distant aspects north and south. Beyond Rum and Eigg, I could just discern the jagged teeth of the Black Cuillin on Skye. Southwards, huge banks of thunder-cloud overhung Islay and Jura—like some Biblical plague held at bay by the Holy Light of Iona. The low November sun was gilding the rolling moor in bands of ethereal light; radiant, yet pregnant with an underlying melancholy bordering on menace, a realm of appalling loneliness. What it must be like in *dreich* weather, or on a chill and deathly night does not bear contemplation! Alas, nowhere in this landscape could I find her cairn.

I must set down a curious incident, or more accurately a curious *thought*, that occurred while I was at the Carn Cul ri Eirinn. I was watching gannets soaring and dive-bombing into the sea, remembering the sparrows and the magnificence of Communion. I was peeling an apple. The penknife slipped, deeply incising my left palm—it bled copiously, onto a patch of pale lichen, discolouring it, spreading in a shape that, ridiculously, resembled a cross. The odd idea came to me that my blood was mingling with the blood of Iona. A sense of ineffability suffused me, as if everything was right, exactly as it should be, ever was and ever shall be. The red ball of the declining sun looked itself like a huge globule of blood, haemorrhaging across a carmine sea. But as it stained the surface of the waters, my elation slowly faded, turning first to awe, then dread, then terror—the panic of the Hebrides.

As I hurried back, I saw another person, a woman, standing on the ridge above the Staonaig Lochan, whom at first I thought (or hoped?) was Mhairi. But by the time I crossed over and began my descent, I could see that it was Ilsa. (I overheard her telling the nuns she tramps the Pilgrims' Path for exercise.) She had made good pace, and was already some way ahead. I was unable to catch up with her. Certainly she is fitter than I. Out here on the moor, even her feather-brained company would have been welcome!

8.30 PM

Mhairi, again, did not seem to be around. I think perhaps she holds some supervisory position, possibly in the kitchen. She cannot be the manager, as that role falls to Fiona, a set-faced Scot in her fifties. I was served by Ilsa. When I tried to make conversation, saying I'd seen her on the moor, she merely smiled inanely. At least I cannot complain about the service tonight. The hotel sources its meat and fish locally. Lobster was on the menu, one of Alida's favourite dishes (though she would have preferred it Thermidor). It was delicious, downed with an excellent Chardonnay, which I imbibed too generously. As I sipped the sparkling wine, my afternoon panic fell into sensible perspective, my mind dwelling rather on those wonderful, euphoric moods that have visited me since I arrived here in Iona. I do not want to leave. Yet tomorrow is my last day. I must enquire whether the hotel has any vacancies. There should not be a problem this time of year.

9.30 PM

Unfortunately, a party of elderly Americans are arriving from Florida, part of an organised tour in search of Scottish ancestry. The hotel is fully booked. Fiona was rather blunt when I enquired about prolonging my stay. "Unusual, for November," she said, as if relishing my disappointment. Perhaps it is as well. In any case, I could not have stood the presence of loud Americans. Fiona has a manner that does not brook small talk, so I stifled the question on my lips about Mhairi. In any case, it might seem indecent, especially these days, for a middle-aged male guest to be enquiring too closely about the young female staff (though I would say Mhairi is a fair bit older than Ilsa).

Wednesday, November 17th
10.00 AM

Today is my final day on Iona. Then back to the real world—that sounds like a cliché, but it has a more exact meaning than anyone might believe who has not *stayed* overnight on Iona (as opposed to day-tripping). To arrive on Iona is to cross a series of borderlines: England to Scotland; Glasgow City, through the Highlands, to the Argyll glens; over the Firth of Lorne to Mull; twenty miles across the mountains, beneath Ben More, along the Ross, then the passage of the Sound of Iona. And there is a spiritual borderline too. At times, these past few days, I have felt I could remain here forever, that I *belonged* on Iona. I am not sure it is a wholesome thought; but if this journal is a record of anything, it is a record of borderlines, and the transgression thereof.

Somebody was in the cemetery as I drew near this morning, soon after dawn. Unable to bear the presence of another there—I feel that M.E.F. is *my* secret—I proceeded to the abbey, where the sparrows swooped and twittered in the nave. I sat awhile in the Chapel of Healing. I watched the rising sun briefly fire its stained glass window, a startling incandescence, illumining the image of a blue Madonna. I say a Madonna, though she is unusual: there is an old prophesy on Iona (which Sharp relates) that here upon this hallowed isle the Redeemer shall return, this time as Bride of Christ, Daughter of God, the Divine Spirit made flesh in Mortal Woman; that "upon the hills, where we are wandered, the Shepherdess shall call us home".

Afterwards, I rested on the stone bench outside St. Oran's, hiding from the westerlies, increasing even in the short spell I was there. I fear the outlook for today is gloomy; the smell of the Atlantic is heavy on the air.

2.00 PM

My plan today has been—and remains—to go back to the moor and make a last attempt to find the cairn. I feel that yesterday I made insufficient effort, that I yielded too easily to a foolish fear, to the loneliness that takes possession all too often in the wilds of the isles. And if I do not go back today, when shall I go? For I do not believe in my heart that once I leave Iona I will return; the island, for all its glory, is fraught with an insidious malaise. No, I shall be relieved to shake it off; and see my experiences here in true perspective—for the insanities they are. Yet, if only I could find the cairn, it would bring a kind of closure. Already afternoon draws in and still I procrastinate. I am torn between compulsion and trepidation.

6.00 PM

I am afraid that my resolve once again deserted me—the weather excuses a multitude of sins here. This afternoon south-westerly gales swept in, a veritable monsoon were it not for their chill. It was impossible even to see across the Sound of Iona. If only I had made the effort first thing, I know, I could have got there. I am aware, glancing through this diary, how often I have allowed the weather to justify delay: in reality, a reluctance born of causes so obscure I can scarcely define them, much less express in words. I dread to cross another borderline. Indefinable, numinous, terrifying.

11.00 PM

I am tempted to attribute this evening's events to a species of predestination, fixed by arcane forces, entreating me, impelling me to remain on Iona. There were two things.

The storms were so bad this afternoon, the ferry did not run. The Americans have been forced to make alternative arrangements (I do not think they even got to

Mull). Fiona brought the news as I was sitting down to dinner. The hotel now has so many vacancies I can stay as long as I like! I heard myself, as if from a distance, agreeing with alacrity—despite a still small voice of protest, for I had just made arrangements to move on to the sybaritic luxuriance of the Manor House in Oban. Fiona herself was waiting at the tables tonight, because "the lasses were away shopping in Bunessan and couldna get back o'er the Sound". This must include Mhairi and Ilsa as the only other waitress was a local girl of about fifteen of singularly limited initiative (a relative, I gather, of Fiona's). The Coq au Vin, when it eventually arrived, was lukewarm—but I am so exhilarated I could not be bothered to complain. I washed it down with several liberal glasses of a fine Italian Merlot.

And more luck! I was reading after dinner a book by Alasdair Alpin MacGregor. In it there was an account of the Fornario case. Though rehearsing familiar ground— in his inimitable style, tragic, wondrous, with a hint of doom—MacGregor offers the most precise clue I have yet seen regarding the location of the cairn. I say "precise" but this is strictly relative. She was not lying anywhere near Dun Lathraichean. It was much closer, near the Pilgrims' Path, not far from where I saw Ilsa. "She lay between the Machair and Loch Staonaig in a hollow in the chilly moor."

Thursday, November 18th
7.30 AM

I have awoken feeling more refreshed than I have done for a long time, though I cannot say my night has been tranquil. I half-awakened several times from unsettling dreams which had about them, nevertheless, a quality of ecstasy, just beyond the brink of recall. They had to do with wandering and being lost, of tribulations and glorious revelations. A chilliness suffused them, as if I were embraced by icy caresses, the cruel, yet kind, caresses of oblivion. But when, sometime before the dawn, I drifted off again, my sleep was deep and rewarding—not since Alida have I slept so pleasingly, as if a loving woman slumbered once again by my side.

10.00 AM

It was scarcely light as I walked up to the Reilig Odhráin. The wind is still in the west, a constant stream of humid air. Overhead, endless billows of featureless grey cloud lour, with dark, low-hanging wisps that oscillate like smoke and weave strange shapes. Briefly, a ghostly sun glimmered, catching the dew-soaked grave, lighting the initials on the open book with an uncanny lustre. *Marie Emily Fornario, I know where they laid you, on the north side of the chapel, domain of unholy death; but today I go to the holy place they found you, where you heard the voices of the angels, where the red sun sets across a hundred isles!*

I watched the coming of the dawn, and felt a vast grace possess me. If I say I scarcely fret about Alida now, that I no longer feel lonely for her, this should not be seen as betrayal of the glory that once was, but an affirmation of the glory that will be. It is still less than a week since I arrived on Iona's sacred shores, "where the far is near, and the dear, far," and already I am transfigured, born into a new dawn by the terrible power of healing. To think that now, at this very moment, I would have been aboard the ferry. I can see it now departing, from my window. Returning to that other world, now fading hourly from my mind.

I have a whole day, endless days, to return to the moor . . .

Friday, November 19th
1.15 AM

I write these words in the knowledge that they may very well be the last I write. It alarms me that eyes other than mine might one day read this journal. Reading through the pages, I am struck by the morbid self-indulgence, the histrionics. It is, in fact, not quite sane. I have toyed with throwing it into the flames, letting them consume my testimony, even as a greater flame consumes my spirit. But I must record the momentous things befalling me today (or, I should now say, yesterday). Before I set forth again tonight, along the Pilgrims' Path, out onto the moor— seventy years to the day since Marie made the same fateful journey—I will hide this journal, unsigned or otherwise identified. There are numberless places in this rabbit-warren of a hotel, with its infinity of old books. One more will not be noticed.

I did not reach the moors until mid-afternoon. I would like to think this time my delay was not so much reluctance, as deferral of a consummation that now felt destined. The wind blew relentlessly, heavy with a scent of rain that never came. The Grey Wind of the West. I made my way to the ground between the Staonaig Lochan and Carn Buidhe, overlooking the Machair. Breakers were crashing all along the wide sweep of the Camus Cul an Taibh, white gulls riding the wind, dipping into the waves, the haunting invocation of their strangled cries calling me as if across immense spaces. Somewhere here, in these few hundred square yards, was the cairn of Marie Emily Fornario.

Even searching so small an area was daunting. Stony intrusions amidst the heather proved, again and again, to be exposed bedrock, without so much as a fragment from which to build a cairn. I searched until the light began to fade. I could feel my spirits plummeting. On the edge of the *lochan* a few lifeless bulrushes shifted in the unceasing grey wind. It was a place of terrible melancholy. As I made to leave, possessed by creeping panic, I experienced a most eerie sensation. I do not find this easy to convey in words. *Déjà vu*? Intuition? Revelation? A series of swift, elusive impressions; a totality, at the heart of which was an overpowering awareness of a *presence*.

I was descending through a depression in the moor—the wind was gusting behind me, great booming surges, buffeting and whistling through the heather—I caught, on the very edge of my vision, like the start of a migraine, a rapid flickering of blue light. I cannot say how long it lasted—fractions of an instant, yet slow and languid; timeless. It was attended by a disconcerting, yet pleasurable, alertness, as before an impending thunderstorm. Though I was temporarily dazzled, I swear I saw ahead of me, silhouetted against the sky, the figure of a tall woman. Her loose, dark hair was flying in the wind. In front of her was a rocky slab, sloping downwards some dozen feet, strewn with loose rubble. Tumbled, forlorn, battered by decades of Hebridean gales, yet still evident, were the remnants of a cairn. They lay in a peat hollow that might once have resembled a cross, overhung with tangled, woody heather. When I raised my eyes again, there was no one—only the vast emptiness of the darkening moor. I replaced several of the fallen stones, and from a wind-blown rowan placed a sprig of crimson berries on the shrine of Marie Emily Fornario.

Soon I will depart, and I am calm, I am consecrated. I no longer feel the pain, the loss, the grief—only exultation. I hear the voices of the angels, summoning me to the moonlit moor. I hear the cry, down the eternal wind, of she who has long been calling me, who has brought Great Healing.

A Golden Dawn will greet us on the Morrow. A New Millennium awaits. Together we shall comprehend a Boundless Splendour, the Splendour of the Light Invisible, the Light Immortal, the Light Inaccessible!

)(

Editor's Note, 3 December 2005

This journal was discovered during the refurbishment in 2005 of the Argyll Hotel, Iona. It takes the form of an A5 ringbound notebook, concealed at the back of a bookcase in the lounge. The proprietor, James Mackay, believed it might shed light on the mysterious disappearance in November 1999 of a Dr. John Campbell; a guest who, having extended his visit, left unannounced without settling his account or taking his baggage. Despite a thorough search of the island, in many places inhospitable and perilous, no body was found; nor have any unidentified bodies been washed up by the sea. The probability remains that Dr. Campbell departed, for reasons best known to himself, on an early ferry, before staff had a chance to notice his absence. Subsequent efforts to locate him proved fruitless; for he never returned to his home in London. It appears, and the journal hints as much, that Dr. Campbell was under emotional stress and was not of sound mind; a view supported by staff who had occasion to deal with him and who considered his behaviour odd. The Fornario case is a piece of local lore that has occasionally drawn unstable interest from those seeking to convey the "weirdness" of Iona. Mrs. Fiona Mackie of Traighmor, whose grandparents boarded Miss

Fornario, denies there is a cairn on the moor, and that, if such ever existed, would long ago have yielded to the elements. Mrs. Mackie was hotel manager at the time of Dr. Campbell's sojourn, and further denies that there was ever anyone working at the Argyll answering to the description, or bearing the name, of Mhairi.

The Light of the World

"It is as if we stood among shadows before a black curtain, as if for one moment a fold were caught back and we saw that which we can never utter: but never deny."

— *Arthur Machen, "Drake's Drum"*

"And while the daring boy in wonder gazed,
Aurora, watchful in the reddening dawn,
Threw wide her crimson doors and rose-filled halls."

— *Ovid,* Metamorphoses

It was the second time Franklyn had encountered the old couple. Once had been enough. It was one of those strange occurrences that seem beyond the bounds of credible coincidence. The incident had enveloped him in a mist of grim foreboding; of precisely what he could not put a name to, but it was no less menacing for being vague. One thing for sure, it had sabotaged any vestige of hope that this trip to the wild north country might resurrect him from the deep depression of the soul that had of late become his daily consort.

A black shadow constantly hovered over him. Although it was seven years since the death of Rowena, enough time one might think to "get over it", the grief had steadfastly refused to dissipate, like the lingering afterglow of a reluctant, fiery sunset. After a fashion, he had started to enjoy life again, and in grand style. He had cruised the Scottish Isles in the perfection of the Hebridean spring. He had journeyed up the Rhine in the joys of Oktoberfest, dizzy from the taste of wines sharp as a blade, basking in the golden radiance of the terraced autumn vineyards. He had been to music festivals at Salzburg, Vienna, and at fabulous expense, Bayreuth. He had taken the Orient Express to Venice, revelling in its incomparable, glorious, decaying elegance.

But this pursuit of exotic avenues of escape, of luxurious compensations, had swiftly ceased to weave its spell. Now, here in the tiny village of Bleng in the foothills of the Cumberland Mountains, he was trying to regain the simple pleasures: walking the fells in the bracing air of late December, playing cards and dominoes with the locals in the Centurion's Arms, drowning his troubles in a few good pints of ale. For many years he had been coming to this lonely valley, staying here beneath the spruce-clad heights of Blengdale Moor. It had become his spiritual home. Here, if anywhere, surely, he would find peace.

As he traversed the emptiness of the moor towards the shelter of the forestry plantation, an icy eastern wind surged and moaned behind him. Blackness enfolded him within her arms, like the surrounding country now disappearing in the winter gloom. Already, though barely three hours past midday, the light was swiftly failing. An hour before, standing upon Colton Heights, looking out across the coastal plane, he had marvelled at the spectacle of the marching monuments of cumulus racing out towards the Irish Sea, back-lit by the brilliant, low-angled beams of the December sun. The old Roman highway over Hard Knott Pass, down towards the ancient fortress of Glannoventa could be clearly seen. Briefly, before tumbling, dark snow clouds draped the fells, the horizontal beams had etched in sharp detail the distant crags of Great Gable. There was nothing, he reflected, like the light of the winter solstice. Ineffable and inaccessible, at times it felt he had almost solved its riddle—glancing on one occasion through the cloisters in Chester Cathedral, on another, shining along the white sands of the Isle of Coll from across the Sea of the Hebrides. It seemed to speak of something beyond the veil.

With twilight's sudden onset the temperatures were falling like a stone, matching his melancholy mood. He wondered whether he had undertaken a walk too ambitious for the weather and the time of day. The forest routes were complex and notoriously deceptive. Old footpaths following natural contours had been displaced by stands of conifers, while the labyrinthine pattern of the plantation roads conformed to no known geographic logic. It was always risky shortcutting through the forest in a hurry and from an unfamiliar direction; in the encroaching dark it was madness—but a lesser evil than the long circuit of the open moor with a blizzard on its way. Around him the huge Norwegian spruces were bending in the wind like ballerinas and howling with strange voices. Loneliness overwhelmed him. He was looking forward to food and drink in the pub, straining his eyes through intermittent forest rides to see if he could glimpse the village lights. But he was probably not yet far enough.

And all the time, though he tried focusing his mind upon the pleasures of the evening ahead, the memory of the strange couple kept coming back to haunt him, as if drawing substance from the burgeoning darkness itself.

Nobody else had seen them. And yet they had made their way down the lane and knocked at Stable Barn in the broad noonday. The village was rarely deserted, and there were some, like Mrs. Stoker from Corner Cottage, who simply never left the house except to brush the steps outside. Johnny Threlkeld, local Jack-of-all-trades, had been working all day long on the vicarage roof, commanding the main street like a sentry in a tower. Enquiries of his immediate neighbours had drawn a blank. "Religious types, did you say?" shouted Mrs. Lamb, who was somewhat deaf, "Not them Jover Witnesses, were they? If I'd opened the door to them I'd 'ave seen 'em on their way, no mistake! And me a good Christian woman! No, love, I never saw no-one."

What he had not told anyone was that he had encountered the same couple some years before—hundreds of miles, and half a continent away—in a small town on the other side of Europe . . .

It had been in the shadowed days soon after the departure of Rowena. Well meaning friends had persuaded him to spend Christmas with them in their apartment on the banks of Lake Lugano in Switzerland. One afternoon when he had remained alone indoors, the weird duo had knocked upon the door. At first he had taken them for gipsies, peddling their wares. But they were bearing the word of God. They were speaking, as far as he could tell, in some Italian dialect. Repeatedly, the woman was making the sign of the cross and other more uncertain gestures, even reaching out to grip him on the shoulder with a lean and bony white hand, decked with gold and silver rings, glistening in the harsh winter light. The only words he could make out were her departing ones: "*Attenti! La Luce del Mondo!*"

He had said nothing about it to his friends. *La Luce del Mondo*. *The Light of the World*. A dreadful, recurring, childhood dream had been rekindled . . .

Franklin came from that generation for whom Sunday school was a customary ritual. Each week the class received an illustrated text-card with an edifying, biblical quotation on one side and a holy image on the other. Invariably sentimental, they typically featured some ecstatic saint, a languid Madonna or a dreamy-eyed, golden-haired Christ. But there was one picture which, for all its maudlin piety, had frightened him. Not until years later would he recognise it as Holman Hunt's famous painting, "The Light of the World". In the picture, a mournful-looking Christ knocks upon a wooden door, clasping in his other hand a shining lantern. Weeds and ivy tangle the entrance, and the background is an eerie landscape with leafless trees stark against the pale light of the dawn. Intended, presumably, to inspire hope at the coming of the light of Christ, in fact it had filled him with horror. The text on the rear declared: "Behold! I stand at the door and knock." Bemused, his mother had sought to reassure him: "But it's only Jesus coming."

The nightmare always took the form of a half-waking dream with an appalling conviction of reality. At first he would find himself in an old, ruined church, the crimson light of dawn silhouetting the broken, stained glass windows. He would walk with leaden feet towards the altar, where a statue of the Madonna looked down upon him with an imponderable smile. Then, in unutterable terror, he would hear the sound he knew was coming: a firm, determined rapping and then the noise of creaking hinges. Relieved, he would seemingly awaken in the security of his own bed—only to find that the bedroom door was slowly swinging open, spreading a widening perimeter of blinding light. Before he witnessed anything more he always wakened. He knew that if he ever did behold what lay behind the door it would be unbearable.

The Light of the World. La Luce del Mondo. And now the couple had returned. They arrived unobtrusively, tapping gently at the door on a morning when a drenching, driving drizzle had marooned him in the cottage. First he saw them as a disembodied blur through the panes of frosted glass in the front door. *Déjà vu?* Every detail was identical, like the umpteenth re-running of a classic film: the outmoded dress, the mumbled words, the dreadful, knowing way they regarded him, deferential and obsequious, yet wily with a secret, smiling triumph. Again they were bearing the Word of God.

The woman, for all her age, looked fit and strong. She was clad in black, a muslin shawl partially obscuring her pale face. Her tangled, dark hair was greying, hanging in unkempt strands across her narrow shoulders. A tarnished silver cross, like the many rings upon her fingers, glittered in the faint daylight. While she was small and lithe, with an almost girlish figure, her companion was tall and gangling, awkwardly stooped as over-tall people often are. He looked older than the woman. His clothes, unsuitable for the inclement weather, spoke of distant climes and summers long ago. In better days he might have graced the first class lounge of a Cunard liner. A few wisps of long grey hair fluttered banner-like from the mottled dome of his head. His grin was inane, almost senile.

The woman did most of the talking, a harsh, almost voiceless rasping, a jumble of Italian and broken English, punctuated at intervals by foolish nodding from the man. It was some kind of religious mumbo-jumbo. There was precious little he could understand. A paralysis of horror seized him. Once again he felt the woman's iron grip upon his shoulder and heard her final words, *"Attenti! La Luce del Mondo!"* She was smiling at him. Somehow, he found the strength to shut the door against them. Looking outside moments later there was no one: only the vast, wintry emptiness of the lane. Flakes of snow were slowly falling. *La Luce del Mondo. The Light of the World.*

Now in the shadow of the forest it was practically night. Only the layers of snow gathering on the ground with an alarming rapidity preserved any remnant of the daylight. Despite the shelter of the trees, a chilling wind was penetrating through; it would not be a night to face outdoors in the wilderness. The prospect of the brightly-lit, smoky bar, the rattle of the dominoes, the laughter and inconsequential chatter of the drinkers shone before him like a beacon. If only he could see the village lights. As he peered through the fluttering snowflakes into the dwindling winter gloom, the landscape was unrecognisable. Either the snow was making everywhere unfamiliar or he was in error as to where he had entered the plantation. By rights he should be veering left, following the downward route out of the forest; but instead he was ascending in a widening curve in the opposite direction. Abruptly, he faced a choice of tracks, but though he gladly seized the turning to the left, this too soon began to curve away.

Thinning trees were revealing a region of extensive, recent timber harvesting. Fighting panic, he stopped and tried to get his bearings. Splintered trunks and tilted trees, many smashed like matchwood, loomed through the cascading snowstorm in mayhem, like the aftermath of some great natural catastrophe. Here and there native broadleaves had been permitted to survive—birch, holly, rowan, gaunt sentinels, emphasising the desolation. Where he was standing must surely be the denuded summit of Blengdale Moor? It was not an encouraging thought. The blizzard was worsening all the time, lashing horizontally across the depredation. In less than half an hour he would be benighted. It had been crazy not to bring a torch. Panic triumphing, he plunged into the debris of the trees, making a beeline in the direction he supposed the way down must lie.

It was as he blundered aimlessly across the devastated moor that Franklyn noticed the large, white signboard. Ten or fifteen feet high, it stood near the top of an exposed, rocky promontory circled by berry-laden hollies. Staggering over fallen logs, he hurried forward, hoping it might be one of the large route maps of the kind on display at the forest entrance. Maybe it marked the summit of the moor, exposed anew by the tree-felling; there was an upright stone on top which looked like a triangulation column. Through the racing snowflakes he could make out bold black lettering. What he read only confused him:

Take the 335 from Florance to Arezzo and thence eastwards on the E78, towards the Appennino-Marchigiano, to Sansepolcro. Twenty kilometres south on the E45 is Città di Castello. Take the Old Mountain Road east for seventeen kilometres into the Valle della Madonna to the village of Santa Maria della Luce. In the churchyard you will see a sign like this giving directions to the sacred place where you are now standing. Beware! The Light of the World!

As Franklyn struggled to comprehend the evidence of his senses, the gale's ferocity intensified, obscuring the sign in whirling flurries. It was like one of those old snowstorm toys he used to love as a child at Christmas, where the glass was shaken and the swirling flakes hid Santa Claus. Despite the gathering intensity of the cold, he was, oddly, almost starting to feel warm again. Happily, his mind roamed back to endless, glorious Christmases. As the twilight dissipated finally, he decided it was time to put out the light and snuggle down beneath the warm, white blankets that Rowena and his mother were spreading so cosily around him. A delicious slumber overwhelmed him . . .

Floating back to consciousness, Franklyn did not know at first where or who he was; for some seconds the very experience of existence seemed incomprehensible. As reality refocused, a dream that had the character of a revelation was hovering on the brink of memory; if only he could grasp it, the very meaning of the universe would be laid bare, its mystery exposed not by reason but by immanence. But swiftly it faded into nonsense. Staring into his face was the grizzled, weather-beaten face of Johnny Threlkeld; he was grinning with relief. Beyond, blending with the white walls of the ward, a stern-faced, middle-aged nurse was writing on a chart held firmly in her hands.

"You were lucky there, lad," said Johnny. "Almost lost you. Another hour and you would've been a goner—hypothermia. What were you doin' up there in that weather? It was only Basil movin' a loggin' truck down to next plantation, otherwise no one would've found you. Not till it were too late, anyway. Aye, you were lucky! We only just got you here in time."

Resting under observation for the next few days, Franklyn had ample time to reconstruct events; but there were blanks and it was difficult in some respects to separate delusion, dream and reality. It was clear, on reflection, that he had been functioning under considerable stress even before the disaster. "Aye, you didn't seem quite right," admitted Johnny under questioning. A swift, anxious look crossed his features when Franklyn mentioned the large, white sign in the woods. Neither Johnny nor anyone he knew had come across such a thing.

"Might be one of them forest sculptures, they call 'em," he added dubiously. "Arty types! Always doin' somethin' daft . . . But most of 'em are away from where you were . . . Unless it was to do with those excavations they're s'posed to be doin' now trees are chopped. Some kind of Roman site or other." He stared silently at Franklyn for a moment. "What I think is, you imagined it. An 'allucination. On account of the cold, like. Basil never said nowt 'bout a sign. Forget it, lad."

But Franklyn could not forget it. The strangest thing was that he could recall with eidetic clarity the directions on the board, burned into his consciousness as if he had been studying a map; not to speak of its enigmatic warning. Nor could he forget about the old couple, though quite possibly that was simply part of the syndrome of delirium—maybe he had dreamed that up as well, a flashback to the incident in Lugano. One thing that bothered him was that they had figured in the elusive, revelatory dream that accompanied his awakening; a dream which, now he thought back to it, was really a variation of the familiar, recurring nightmare.

And over the following days, usually when he was emerging from sleep, flashes of the dream, for millionths of a second, would sear his mind, simultaneously terrifying and glorious, connected in some way with a great empty void and a bright, shining light.

※

When one day he went out and bought a map of Italy, Franklyn knew he was approaching a moment he had been putting off for months.

Whatever the provenance of the sign, it was immediately obvious its directions were accurate. First he located

Florence, scanning to the right to find the Apennines. They were subdivided into individual ranges. There was the Appennino-Marchigiano, maybe seventy miles to the south-east. An uneasy prickling ran up his neck as he located, like a child joining up the dots in a picture-puzzle, the names of the towns: Arezzo, Sansepolcro, Città di Castello. Searching to the right, where the contours narrowed, he found what he was looking for: in the tiny lettering reserved for the least significant places on the map, at the end of a twisting hill road into the Valle della Madonna, was Santa Maria della Luce.

Northern Italy was in the grip of a ferocious heat wave when, towards the end of June, Franklyn arrived in Florence; at least it was better than the rain-drenched gloom of Manchester Airport. His lodgings were economical and comfortable, quite centrally located, run by a large, noisy family, possessed, though, with only a smattering of tourist English. Lacking all but a few restaurant and travel phrases himself, conversation proved somewhat limited, though more than compensated by the excess of joviality. But he was unable to find out anything concerning his destination in the mountains. He was, however, already booked as far as Città di Castello by a series of road and rail links, stamped with the imprimatur of Thomas Cook.

Perambulating round the galleries and churches of Florence proved an enervating experience, and he was not in best shape to appreciate the masterpieces in the crowded Uffizi Gallery, which he had waited, so to speak, a lifetime to see; it had been on Rowena's list of the many things they'd planned to do—before the tragedy. The furnace-like temperature made him queasy. And at the forefront of his mind, constantly, preventing him from really enjoying things, was his uncertain quest. What did he expect to find? Even if he had felt able to explain to his convivial hosts the object of his trip, they would surely have regarded him with blank incomprehension.

His onward journey proved a nightmare. The neatly printed, computer travel itinerary, listing the various timings and connections, proved to be little more than a wish list. The punctuality of the trains had clearly deteriorated since Mussolini's day, but at least the timetable bore some degree of credibility; the bus links, however, seemed to operate in accordance with a completely different order of reality. Consequently, he was forced into an unscheduled overnight stop in Sansepolcro, in a seedy tavern where noisy guests below drank all night long and large insects stalked and flitted on the bedroom walls.

Fortunately, at Città di Castello the hotel had held his booking. The journey there was stifling but, despite the purgatorial conditions, the beauty of the light and landscape, as the long, midsummer evening drew to a close, transfixed him. It was close to the summer solstice. As he surveyed the pellucid, greenish-golden light percolating through the tangled olive groves and vineyards, it was as if he were entering the mysterious, luridly coloured background to an old Tuscan painting. What had previously seemed to him—denizen of a grey, cloud-wreathed, northern island—as artistic license and fanciful exaggeration was here revealed as the expression of an uncanny verisimilitude.

Città di Castello, an ancient walled town, itself resembled the scenery from an old master. In contrast to the places he had so far passed through—like Arezzo, which, despite its fame as the birthplace of Vasari and Piero della Francesca, and its elegant Gothic cathedral, proved a faceless, modern city—Città di Castello made Franklyn feel that here at last he was entering the world of the real

Italy. The clustered towers and spires, the labyrinth of narrow streets and alleys, seemed scarcely changed since the days of Giotto. The lingering radiance in the west, as a glorious sun declined behind ruby-rimmed lineaments of cloud, fitfully lightening the hills with golden fire, conjured images of Sistine Chapel angels reaching down from Paradise. Eastwards, on a rocky promontory above the Tiber, loomed the city fortress—like battlements of fire in a scene by Turner. And beyond, receding endlessly, it seemed, into the far distance, soared the undulating heights of the Appennino-Marchigiano, saturated in a terrible, fiery glow.

The Hotel Mantegna, a modest establishment with a fascinating air of fading elegance, was on the main piazza. A balcony off his room afforded a sweeping panorama across a forest of church towers and angled roofs. Though still not entirely dark, stars were already twinkling with a pale, ethereal effulgence. In spite of the aggressive heat, the air felt lighter here and fresher than any he had breathed since touching down at Florence Airport. The continental brouhaha coming from the piazza and the squalling of feral cats reminded him he was far from home. Loneliness possessed him. The young hotel staff spoke English passably well, but the waiter was vague when he enquired about directions to Santa Maria della Luce. "You speak to the manager, signore, he comes from the mountains."

Signor Moretti, a thick-set man in his fifties with a mane of steel-grey hair, was pleased to chat with an Englishman. He and his family were ardent Anglophiles, frequently holidaying in Windermere, where his brother ran a restaurant. Fortified by the heady local wine, a friendship was quickly established. Signor Moretti came from Camerino further south, not far from Perugia.

"Santa Maria della Luce," he repeated quizzically, "I go there once as a boy. *Un luogo strano* . . . A strange place.

Very beautiful. A tiny valley. There was a miracle there. Many years ago. The Madonna!" He gave a short laugh, "But she is appearing in many places, ha! ha! There is an old church. It looks east . . . on, er, a great rock, a great hill . . . out towards Monte Catria. It is maybe twenty kilometres? Take one of the hotel's cars. It will be a pleasure, signore!"

Franklyn awoke late next morning feeling unrefreshed; heat, travel and the missed connections had imposed their toll. But there was no rush, he told himself; he could go tomorrow. Now he had arrived at the threshold of his destination, a certain restlessness urged him on, but equally a curious apprehension was besieging him; though this, he assured himself, was not the reason for his procrastination. According to Signor Moretti, the town was well worth exploring, with a treasury of art by the masters rivalling the Vatican. Over breakfast he perused the tourist brochure provided by the hotel, detailing the sights of the town and its rural environs.

Città di Castello was noted for its fine Romanesque cathedral and several magnificent Renaissance palaces built by the city's fifteenth century magnates, the Vitellis. In La Cappella della Maddalena there were frescos, albeit in very damaged condition, by Piero della Francesca, depicting twenty-eight scenes from the life of St. Francis of Assisi. In Santo Spirito was the only known surviving section of the Botticini altarpiece, reputedly banished from the Vatican when its patron, Matteo Palmieri, was accused of heresy for alleging human souls to be the angels who stayed neutral when Lucifer rebelled. A troubling crucifixion by Masaccio, that once hung in Pisa Cathedral, could be seen in the Palazzo Ducati. Skimming through the pages dealing with the surrounding countryside, the name, Santa Maria della Luce, caught his eye:

Santa Maria della Luce, situated in the beautiful Valle della Madonna, in the heart of the Appennino-Marchigiano, is famous for its vineyards and its mineral springs, and for an apparition of the Madonna seen in 1925 by a mentally disturbed, fourteen year old girl, Trina Scalza. The vision appeared at dawn on the rocky outcrop where the ancient church from which the village takes its name still stands. Staring hard into the rising sun, in her efforts to apprehend the vision, blinded her for life; but she went forth and brought great light and healing to the world. She is reputed to have lived to a great age, though no one knows where she lies; superstition has it that she still walks abroad, accompanied by her guardian, spreading to those in troubled mind the glory and terror of the light. It was also on this site, before the coming of Christianity, that the Romans and their predecessors worshipped the coming of the dawn and made tribute to Aurora. The church is currently cordoned off for restoration, following an earth tremor in 1999, rendering the structure unsafe and damaging works of art. Amongst these is a fresco of Christ in the Garden of Gethsemane, which some experts believe to be by Cimabue himself, not a follower; if true, it is possibly the earliest example of Florentine art in the land. Santa Maria della Luce is dedicated specially to those suffering from mental anguish and spiritual malaise, as Christ suffered in Gethsemane and, indeed, as Trina Scalza herself suffered before she was blessed with the visitation of Our Lady.

Franklyn wondered whether to change his plans and go immediately. The reference to the restoration work, certainly, was not encouraging; but the brochure, he noted, was dated 2000, and by now the work might be complete. In the end inertia ruled and he passed the morning sampling the city's estimable art treasures. At the manager's insistence, he joined Signor Moretti for lunch at the hotel's piazza café. A cooling breeze was blowing off the mountains, and after several glasses of the region's best vintage red, courtesy of the Hotel Mantegna, he felt his spirits rising. He spent a pleasing afternoon strolling by the river, languidly imagining its weaving course, past the towered hills of Perugia, down through the lakes of Umbria and on to Rome and the Tyrrhenian Sea.

Re-entering the city walls later that day, a relaxing evening beckoned. He was looking forward to indulging further in the hotel's excellent cuisine and friendship over wine with his host. The world was moving back into reassuring perspective; a trip tomorrow into the hills would do him good. A cool shower and a bracing *apéritif* on his balcony were the immediate priorities.

Franklyn did not know why he suddenly decided to cross the piazza and enter the maze of alleys sloping down towards the west. Perhaps it was the declining sun, glancing across the spires and roof tops, that lured him. The area was bustling and crowded, patronised mainly by the local youth. There were frequent taverns and pizzerias, laughter and music in the air, a frenetic energy radiating through the atmosphere like electricity. Suddenly he felt out of place, aware of his age, wishing he had stayed at the hotel. A group of boisterous, drunken girls bounced him aside; their indifference was more disconcerting than hostility. He shaded his eyes against the sun, which seemed to spin dazzlingly before him.

It was the old man he saw first, betrayed by his unusual height and the incongruity of his years amidst the youthful pandemonium.

Franklyn heard the woman's rasping voice before the grip descended on his shoulder: "*Attento! La Luce del Mondo!*"

The powerful wrist was pulling him, forcing him around to confront his dread molester. The tall old man was muttering inanely. Crowds swelled about, jostling them, oblivious, whirling the trio along the alley in a carousel of horror. Spots from the setting sun swam before Franklyn's eyes. The woman's face was thrust right into his; he could see that her teeth were rotten and smell the foulness of her breath. Flakes of skin were peeling from her gaunt cheek bones. Her expression was exultant, terrifying. For the first time Franklyn realised she was blind.

Shaking himself free of the vise-like grasp, he escaped and ran pell-mell through the surging crowds, heedless of collision. At one corner he overturned a table, shattering a carafe of wine in the gutter, angry voices following him. At last he came to the cathedral, glimmering red in the dying rays of the sun. Beyond lay the sanctuary of the hotel, its crumbling façade reflecting back the eerie glow. *La Luce dello Mondo*.

Somehow he composed himself sufficiently to eat something, liberally washed down with a harsh Chianti. He spent a fitful night, endlessly disturbed by nightmares and the chiming from the many bell-towers. The evening he had passed alone, Signor Moretti having been called away on business to Foligno; he could have used the company. As often happens after excess alcohol, he awoke too early, unable to get back to sleep.

Darkness still reigned as he departed the hotel in the battered Fiat pick-up truck loaned by his host. The skies were heavy as he took the narrow, winding road up into the hills. Yesterday's pleasant breeze had disappeared; already it was humid, later it would scorch. High up in the hills thunder boomed.

The first hints of a fiery dawn were appearing above the mountains by the time the rattling vehicle turned up into the Valle della Madonna. The high peaks of the Appennino-Marchigiano were tearing through the veil of the night clouds, their distant flanks touched by the slightest tint of rose, as he pulled into Santa Maria della Luce. The village was almost at the valley head, road signs indicating a dead end for motorists. A hikers' sign, beside a large crucifix, pointed towards the Col dell'Alba. There were few people abroad at this early hour. The village clustered around three rugged, pine-clad rocky outcrops, the tallest prominently surmounted by the ancient church. Abandoning the truck, Franklyn climbed the steep, twisting lane, past ugly, maudlin Stations of the Cross, driven by an urgency he did not really understand. His quest, pointless as it seemed on cool reflection, was almost complete.

The ancient church perched precariously on the far edge of the hill, which on its further side was little more than a crumbling cliff face, as if a great blade had severed what had once been a rounded summit. Stunted pine and gorse studded the terrain, while on the distant slopes beyond climbed acres of vineyards. A high, metal fence encircled the area, notices repeatedly declaring: *Pericolo. Ingresso vietato.*

At considerable risk, Franklyn squeezed his way around the fence, where the fence terminated at the cliff's edge. The heavens were lightening to a glowing pink but still the sun was hidden by the peaks. The church of Santa

Maria della Luce stood gaunt before him, its tiny cemetery enclosed by spiked railings. The rusting gate was padlocked but a section of collapsing railing allowed him entrance. Ancient graves with tilted, lichen-coated monuments loomed. Strips of moss dangled from distorted shrubs. Faceless angels beckoned. The building was clamped with scaffolding and there were signs that restoration, in some desultory fashion, was still in process.

On the great white hoarding, which he half hoped was another danger sign or something to do with the restoration work, were printed in bold black lettering the following words:

> Procedendo lungo l'autostrada da Lancaster, prendi la A595 e poi la A5092 fino a Duddon Bridge. Prendi la salita di Ulpha verso Muncaster e la vecchia strada romana verso Hardknott Pass. Cinque miglia ad ovest, lungo la strada che è l'entrata per la Foresta di Blengdale, vedrai un cartello come questo con le indicazioni stradali per raggiungere il santuario dove ti trovi adesso. Attenti! La luce del Mondo!

Franklyn felt like an actor playing out a familiar script as he walked towards the church and stepped inside. Within, the crimson light of dawn was silhouetting the broken, stained-glass windows. He walked with leaden feet towards the altar, where a statue of the Madonna looked down upon him with an imponderable smile. In unutterable terror he waited for the sound he knew was coming. A firm, determined rapping echoed round the church and hinges loudly creaked. A wooden door to the left of the altar, in an angle of the wall, was slowly opening, spreading a widening perimeter of light. He stumbled towards the doorway and gazed out into the glory of the dawn.

The brilliance of the rising sun was splintering like a starburst on the distant peak of Monte Catria. A laser beam of light, one hundred and eighty-six thousand miles per second, lit up the church of Santa Maria della Luce like a supernova. In the millionth of a second before his sight was scorched Franklyn knew the ending of his dream.

What he saw, out there beyond the door, made him glad that all his eyes would ever see again was darkness.

)(

On Blengdale Moor three figures watched the ambulance ply its way slowly through the debris strewn across the forest track.

"Don't get it!" exclaimed Johnny Threlkeld, "No-one knew 'e were 'ere. Not been in pub. Not stayin' anywhere. No car. No nothin'!"

He turned to the young, blond-haired archaeologist. "How did you come to find 'im, love?"

Dr. Thulin, of the Anglo-Swedish Archaeological Society, gestured vaguely back across the moor. "I am here on a placement. I waked up early to come here and see the dawn. I saw him over there." Again she pointed vaguely into the devastation, "It is strange. At first I think he is with two other people. But, actually, when I get closer he is alone. Simply staring! I am not sure he is alive, so I call the police on my mobile."

"Where 'bouts did you see 'im, love?" asked Basil. "Exactly, like."

"I am telling you," she replied impatiently, "Over there! On that rocky outcrop with the holly trees."

Johnny and Basil exchanged quick glances. "That's where you found 'im last winter, ain't it?" said Johnny.

Basil nodded, then looked at Dr. Thulin again. "You're absolutely sure it was on that hillock, love?" he said, slowly. "By that standing stone?"

"Well, yes!" she snapped. "But it is not a standing stone, actually. It is what our dig is about. It is Roman masonry. Part, we think, of a temple to Aurora, goddess of the dawn." She looked towards the eastern horizon, shading her eyes. "I was here very early. As you can see, it is a glorious place to watch the morning coming over the Great Gable."

An American Writer's Cottage

"Then he walked out upon the moonlit grass; and at the ford he saw a woman stooping and washing shroud after shroud of woven moonbeams: washing them there in the flowing water, and singing low a song he did not hear."

– *Fiona Macleod,* The Washer of the Ford

It was the island's extremity of isolation that appealed to Margaret. At least that was what she thought at first. Arriving late on a cold, grey day in April, the gloom of the scene was pronounced. Fleeing a particularly dire set of professional and personal circumstances, she had chosen to escape to as inaccessible a place as she could find. Dr. Margaret Orde, lecturer in literature at the University of Oxford and denizen of smart suburbia, preferred her wilderness, like her whisky, neat.

On a rickety wooden quay, at the end of the twisting, woody lane from Acharacle, she awaited the island's owner. MacBeath arrived in a capacious rowing boat, personally ferried across the narrow stretch of water, an arm of the Hebridean seas; a gaunt, angular figure, plying his way against a sluggish ebb-tide. Emerging indistinctly from the gloom, his hunched spectacle called to mind Charon crossing the Styx. He was attired in rough working clothes. Margaret might well have taken him for one of the estate workers, had the woman's voice on the phone not advised her that it would be her husband, the laird himself, who would meet her.

Shuna was not an island she had ever heard of until, browsing a walkers' magazine for a secluded cottage, she had seen the advert. Shuna Estates offered holiday lets in a number of such dwellings; on an isle, moreover, with no roads, indeed without motor access, except for estate vehicles It was a veritable haven as far as Margaret was concerned. Cars, explained the brochure, could be left safely alongside the quay. The fate of her aging Vauxhall was a matter of little concern to her; though abandoning it (the only one there) in the grey afternoon, as she awaited the boat, left her with a hollow feeling. It was, she reflected, a threshold; and it made her ponder, not for the first time here in the isles, on the frailty of civilisation and our craven dependence on its trappings.

Margaret scrutinised her host as he deftly conducted the arcane manoeuvres necessary to secure the vessel, bobbing in the restless tide. A woolly hat obscured his face, pulled down low against the unseasonable icy breeze—if unseasonable was the right word for the fickle Scotch weather—but she noted his bold, square jaw. He had a robust and tall physique, an authoritarian bearing which spoke plausibly of Scottish aristocratic ancestry. He could have been anywhere in his late fifties or sixties, eminently fit. There was about him a distinctly military aspect, and she surmised (rightly, as it turned out) an earlier career in a prestigious Scottish regiment. When he spoke—a man of few words—it was with an educated, almost English intonation. His voice, neither impolite nor unfriendly, was expectant, nevertheless, of natural obedience.

"Miss Orde?" He limply shook her hand. "MacBeath." His eyes were a piercing blue, his expression formal and correct, yet there was in it an aspect she could not quite fathom: a preoccupation maybe, a suggestion of a more troubled man beneath the pose of aplomb, a man with something on his mind.

"Is this all your luggage?" he asked, without waiting for a reply. "All aboard then—and mind the quay, it's slippery."

Margaret nodded. She shouldered the bulky rucksack, handing him her commodious travel bag and the clinking cartons of supermarket fare. Milk and eggs had been arranged in advance, but she had been advised to bring generous provisions; the nearest shop was at Acharacle. She faced her taciturn host as he rowed his way back to the pine-shrouded island, a dark silhouette against the fading western light.

"Am I the only one?" she asked, breaking the awkward silence. She glanced back to her solitary motorcar. A flurry of wind, bringing with it a sharp blast of sleet, drowned his exact words.

She lent forward quizzically.

"Pardon?"

"I said, 'First guest of the season'."

"How many cottages are there?"

"Four," he replied. "There's a couple more for staff—and one gone to ruin." No doubt he had seen her backward glance, for he added, "Your car will be all right there."

They alighted at a small jetty. Shadowy pines enclosed them, stealing the remnants of the afternoon; at least they shielded them against the wicked breeze. A curious mood had descended on Margaret, eroding the exhilaration of arrival. Second thoughts about the wisdom of staying in so solitary a place assailed her. She thought with a pang of earlier holidays with Frank. It was not that she felt afraid, or anything like that; but there was about the island a feeling of foreboding, a palpable, troubling loneliness.

A light twinkled through the darkling trees, a welcome beacon in the wild. An enticing tang of wood-smoke wafted down.

MacBeath roughly dumped her wares—she winced—in the back of a hardy farm vehicle, a tractor of some type. As they swayed and bumped along the stony track he explained arrangements. They were passing the house with the light, a stone structure like a manse with high, narrow gables.

"Shuna House. Where we live," he said. "Your place is further on. A quiet little bay. It's a wood fire, logs in the annexe, there should be plenty. Milk and eggs in the fridge. Stove runs on Calor Gas, just replenished. So, as long as you're not cooking a turkey dinner every night it should last."

The track descended, clearing the pines. Here the sky looked brighter. A smudge of turquoise-green stained the west; tattered veils of shifting, smoky cloud wove elegant tracery upon it. Craggy slopes rose sheer to the left. The splashing of a tumbling burn cut through the engine's drone. The cottage nestled in a shallow dell amidst dense rhododendrons, low and practical-looking, daubed in a faded whitewash. Not far beyond was the loch, darkly rippling in the dusk. Margaret felt perturbed, disquieted. Depression's monstrous wings fluttered over her. What she needed was a drink.

MacBeath briskly pointed out the fairly obvious facilities and the wood-store. "If you need anything call at the house."

As he walked away he turned, "Oh! And make sure the fire's damped down when you go to bed. We had one burn down."

Margaret watched the vehicle trundle back into the pines until the sound of its engine faded. Only the tinkling stream, rippling over the track into a steep declivity in the garden, and the call of a curlew on the shore broke— or rather reinforced—the silence. There was an icy edge to the air; it caught her breath as she inhaled a cigarette. Shivering, she took herself gratefully to the glowing logs, lit in readiness for her arrival, stoking the fire to a blaze. On an impulse she could not explain, perhaps simply a wish for cosiness, she drew the curtains over the small sash-window that looked to the loch, now descending into gloom.

Exploration of the cottage was a matter of minutes. A tiny porch led into a vestibule, right of which was a small parlour; ahead was a diminutive kitchen; to the left, the bedroom, with a shower in a cupboard-like alcove. An assortment of slightly tatty furniture cluttered the house, surfaces arrayed with embroidered fabrics, knick-knacks and sundry treasures from the shore. A pleasant fragrance pervaded, of sea, sand and smouldering wood—and another scent she could not quite identify. A door in the parlour, which looked as if it might lead to another room, led into the wood-store.

Exhausted by her journey—Scottish miles were long and tedious—she made do with a light meal, washed down with a liberal glass of the Famous Grouse, hoping MacBeath had not identified the source of the clinking heaviness in her bags. Still, this was Scotland, it was hardly unusual here. It was a little past half-nine when she retired, glad to collapse beneath the sheets, musty though they were.

Margaret did not arise until nine the following morning. She recalled an uneasy dream in which she lay partly conscious, aware of a noise she thought to be coming from behind the door to the wood-store. It was a sound—

more than a sound, a vibration—as of something heavy falling. What was so disturbing about the dream was that it had felt as if it were really happening; as if she had awoken amidst the misty realms of weariness and whisky, wanting to get up, yet unable to make the physical effort, then drifting off again. The recollection was sufficiently niggling for her, once up and about, actually to check the wood-store.

The space, to judge from the presence of a fireplace and a small window, had once been part of the dwelling. There were logs to last many months, an abundance of kindling lay in a corner, and bundles of newspapers wrapped in black plastic bags against the damp. There were crates, bottles, boxes, the assemblage of junk typically littering such places. A further door gave access to the exterior. She tried the handle; it was fastened from within, the key rusted in the lock. There were no signs of anything untoward. Nevertheless, a shiver passed through her. The place was dismal. It felt chilly after the parlour, where the scented warmth of last night's logs pleasantly lingered.

Meandering outside, smoking the first cigarette of the day, she approached the loch. A stretch of grass, broken here and there with white quartz boulders, swept down to a pebbled strand. A few sparse daffodils wavered in the cold breeze. The distance to the other shore could not have been more than a few hundred yards. Beyond, austere slopes loomed. Was it Moidart or Knoydart? Or Morvern? The black intervening waters lent the place, even in the fair morning light, an aspect of the sinister, a disquieting melancholy. Margaret shuddered as the nicotine coursed through her veins.

Coming from the loch was a sound which she realised she had been subconsciously aware of since stepping outside; an eerie moan, rising and falling in the morning clarity, a mournful ululation, yet a voice of haunting beauty. Then she saw them: grey Atlantic seals, four or five, their heads protruding inquisitively from the water, staring at her with their large humanlike eyes; and several more along the shore. Margaret thought of the Selkie legends, the seal-people. Encountering them here in the wilderness, hearing their lamentations, there was about it all somehow nothing sentimental; it partook too much of the uncanny. She retreated, shivering, back to the cottage and set about breakfast.

The modest tot of whisky on her porridge, she told herself, was a good old Scottish custom. It livened up the coffee too. Today, she decided, lighting another cigarette, she would take things easy, get the feel of her environs, settle into her abode. First, she tried to locate her position on the Ordnance Survey map. Annoyingly, the northern tip of Shuna, where the cottage stood, was just clipped off. There was a mark on the cusp of the map that might conceivably be hers but it looked too close to Shuna House. The loch and mainland were missing too. She lacked the next map north. It only showed the treachery of dividing Scotland into neat compartments. Westwards, where the loch turned south, the north shore reappeared. A path encircled the island.

Margaret had not proceeded far when she came upon the ruins of an old chapel, roofless, with walls intact. Briefly, she lingered in its environs, sensing the loneliness of lost communities. The path continued through broom, birch and gorse, following the contour of the coast, petering out on a short peninsula. The islands of the west lay before her, strangely near, dusted in the snow of early spring: Eigg and Muck, the hills of Rum, every crag and cranny etched in crystal perfection, like a chiaroscuro print. Beyond, across a shining sea, she could see the Isle of Skye, the jagged Coolin peaks whiter still, a mirage of a far-off land in a fairy tale. Margaret smoked, taking in the beauty, and wept for all that she had lost, resting a quarter of an hour until the cold forced her to move.

Returning—she felt too exhausted to go further today—Margaret saw, not far from the chapel, a building she had not noticed on her outward journey. It lay close by the water's edge. That, too, could await the morrow.

Margaret spent the afternoon pottering, arranging and rearranging her things. There was a pungent scent in the wardrobe—the indefinable scent of last night. Perfume of some kind, or incense? The 1970s flashed back: patchouli oil—was that still used? Whoever had used the wardrobe last must have fairly flung it about. Hadn't MacBeath said she was the season's first guest? In a kitchen cupboard she found a chipped crystal glass with a slender stem. She emptied the contents of her half-drunk mug of Chablis into the glittering receptacle, swishing the golden fluid round. It had been a mistake not to bring more wine, but she had worried about the weight. By the time she had finished her third glass she was ready to lounge before the fire. It was nice, with the extra hour, to watch the daylight linger.

She dozed, and when she wakened evening had settled in: the window gaped, a black maw. She got up and drew the curtain. More logs were needed. She approached the wood-store, listening, the silence broken only by the crackling fire. Taking a torch, cagily she undid the bolt. At first the light failed to work, flat batteries, she feared; but, fumbling, she got it on, relieved as its pure white light cleansed the gloom. She conducted a fuller search than in the morning; though quite what she was expecting to find—or hoping not to find—she could not have said. The sweeping rays lit up tangled webs, hanging from a high beam that ran the roof's length. Behind the log pile she came upon some old bottles. Famous Grouse! Someone shared the same good taste—or the same problem. There were empties, too, of vodka, gin and brandy, and several kinds of wine.

Cobbling together a meagre supper, Margaret found in the knife-drawer a booklet of instructions about the dwelling—evidently named Rowan Cottage. In the same plastic folder were notes on the island and a crude map. These she perused by the fire. The instructions puzzled her, seeming not properly to relate to the cottage. Curiously, it was said to have a dining room as well as a parlour; this, she presumed, must have become the wood-store. Shuna House dated from the eighteenth century, rebuilt in the 1880s. The chapel had been in use by the Free Church of Scotland until 1961; and there had once been a school, latterly used for the corralling of rams during the winter. Rhododendrons and exotics from the Himalayas had naturalised on the island, and palms thrived in the Gulf Stream. Rare geese visited, especially at the spring and autumn equinoxes, and so on . . .

It all sounded interesting enough; once it would have thrilled her more. Though pleased with the seclusion, somehow it all felt wrong. A deep loneliness possessed her. She thought, as she opened another bottle of Grouse, of all the good times with Frank, on Arran, Mull, Skye . . . but it did no good to brood. And was it merely despondency she felt? More than that—a species of malaise, a distressing wariness, a sense of trepidation, as if something awful were about to happen.

She turned her attention to the map. The path around the island was roughly delineated. The chapel was indicated by a cross. The holiday cottages were marked, all named after trees. There were a few other buildings, all unidentified—except for one. It appeared to be not far away from her own, described intriguingly as "a cottage sometimes occupied by an American writer". The isle, she reflected, would be a fine place to write. Was this, then, the building she had noticed on her walk back yesterday?

Margaret set aside the pages. She stacked more logs on the fire, succumbing to the lulling apathy of whisky. When the flames died, she prepared for bed. My God, could the new bottle have gone down so far? On a last impulse she dragged an armchair against the wood-store door.

A thumping headache greeted her in the morning. It was not yet six. She surveyed herself in the faded mirror— the morning light was unflattering, but there were worse things. At least it was a lovely day outside. Fluffy clouds drifted in a saffron sky. The wind was cool, yet with a freshness redolent of spring. Odd flakes of snow blustered, the perennial battle of the Scottish seasons. In an old lone rowan sparrows flitted, and a hoodie stalked the shore. There was no sign of the seals today.

Margaret suddenly felt, uncannily, as if she were being watched. She cast her eyes about in a wide sweep. Slowly, she approached the cottage, circuiting it like a wary animal, even stepping from the dell and surveying the track. Or was the sensation emanating from behind? It seemed to swing about, like an elusive echo, impossible to locate with precision, eventually dissipating.

Loneliness. That was all.

After breakfast she packed some lunch and set out on an exploration of the island, taking the opposite direction from yesterday. By Shuna House a middle-aged woman was tethering a black and white border collie. It growled unpleasantly at Margaret.

"Don't worry about him. He won't bite," the woman said, regarding the creature indulgently, "A bad tempered so-and-so, aren't you?"

The dog lunged angrily, still growling.

"Quiet! Charlie! Quiet!" Her voice was stern. Charlie submitted to authority: a sharp lash from the long leash the woman was reining in.

"You'll be staying at the cottage? I'm Catriona. We spoke on the phone. Is everything all right there?" She held out her free hand. She spoke with the attractive lilt of the west.

Margaret was glad of a conversation, and her hostess appeared friendly, someone she could get along with.

"Margaret." she announced.

"Now, you're sure you're all right down there?"

They exchanged pleasantries. The weather, she had discovered years ago, provided an endless fund of conversation up here. Shuna, Catriona was explaining, had its own climate; even the local weather forecast was unreliable. A friend in Acharacle had rung to say there was a blizzard—and that not ten miles away.

"But we like it, we wouldn't have it any other way. We came here twelve years ago, when Alex left the Black Watch. The estate's been in his family since the eighteenth century. The upkeep of a place like this nowadays—you wouldn't believe!"

Catriona laughed. She was a handsome woman, the wrong side of fifty, Margaret suspected, but well-preserved. She was tallish and slim, a little bit dowdy, not the kind of wife she would have expected of a military man. She looked Hispanic, with jet black hair tied loosely back in a ponytail. She had glittering dark eyes, thin lips and an aquiline nose. She came from Tobermory.

"I was passing by just now, but didn't like to intrude. We're fetching more milk tonight and we wondered if you wanted any? And anything else? Alex is taking the jeep down to Fort William tomorrow, so we'll do a big shop."

Margaret hesitated. She couldn't very well ask for booze to be delivered. Catriona looked askance. "Well," she said, "yes, some milk, and butter and, er . . . any chance of a bottle of wine? I, er . . . was going to cook something special, and I forgot to buy . . . Er, white, a couple of bottles? . . . If that's all right?"

"Of course it is!" declared Catriona, knowingly. "I'll get you something decent. We've got a cellar here. Good stuff. None of that supermarket plonk."

"I'm sure it will suffice," laughed Margaret.

"That's done," said Catriona brightly. "Chardonnay okay? I'll drop it in at the cottage and add it to your account?"

Margaret climbed steeply into the woods behind the house, following a short cut Catriona had indicated to the top. She felt out of breath, unfit. To think she had once climbed Sgurr nan Gillian in the Coolin. That was with Frank, who hated smoking. It was too late now; it was one of the few pleasures left. Eventually, she emerged above the treeline on a rolling tableland of rock and heather.

Bleak hills extended many miles inland. In the foreground she could see the road to Acharacle disappearing into woods; there was the pier—and her car. She perceived it with a vague sense of unreality, as if she were staring into an abyss of time. She tried to pick out her cottage, tracing her eyes left along the coastline. At last she spied it: concealed within its shrubby dell, a corner of the roof just visible. Efforts to find a better perspective were foiled by the rough terrain. Nature, as usual in Scotland, abhorred a straight line.

Margaret was forced to detour considerably. After a while a new aspect opened up; alarmingly one of utter unfamiliarity. She noticed another cottage. Could this be the one occupied by the American writer? It was situated on a small bay, with a burn running through a narrow ravine to the shore. A woman with long untidy hair, in a whitish smock, was engaged in some indefinable chore. Was this the mysterious writer? Margaret had assumed the writer to be female, quite why she could not say.

But, no—recognition came with a shock—the cottage she was looking at was none other than her own. For some seconds this very recognition discomposed her. She was seized by a species of vertigo.

Who, then, could this woman be? Whoever it was had now gone. The thought of an intruder was troubling. The memory was strangely vague, like a vision in a mist. Was it Catriona? After all, she had business there, delivering the wine. Nevertheless, it might be worth asking if anyone else were about on the island. She recalled her earlier feeling of being watched, though probably that had been Catriona too—she said she had been passing. Seeking privacy, Margaret felt dismayed at the prospect of its violation.

She settled down in the heather in a welcome patch of sun and ate her roll, washing it down with a crude dry sherry. This might be supermarket plonk, as the laird's wife put it, but these miniatures were ideal for a picnic.

Margaret slept, awaking uneasily. She was cold. Grey cloudbanks spanned the west, merging land and sea. The islands hovered like a mirage. The moor looked uninviting. Instead of continuing as planned, she went back the way she had come.

Catriona was working in the garden, pruning an unkempt laurel hedge. She hailed Margaret. "This grows like mad, even in winter. I was just making tea, would you be joining me in a cup?"

Margaret assented. Her mouth was parched; at least it was liquid. Luckily, the dog was not about. She could hear its irascible barking at the rear of the house, and MacBeath telling it to shut up.

Catriona took her into a small room with a disproportionately high ceiling. Despite the tall windows, it was rather dark. It had a disorderly air, and again Margaret wondered that its mistress should be a guardsman's wife. There was too much furniture, creating a cluttered effect. Chairs and sofas were covered in a frayed violet brocade, worried by claws. MacBeath came in, dressed in overalls. He nodded abruptly.

Catriona returned with a laden tray. To Margaret's relief her hostess lit a cigarette, offering her one. Mutual grumbles were exchanged about the recent ban on smoking in public places, the new Puritans.

Margaret's confidence grew. "Who's the American writer?"

Catriona looked nonplussed.

"In your guidebook, the little map." Margaret persisted, "She stays in a cottage here?"

"Oh! Gosh! Is that stuff still there?" Catriona eyed her quizzically. "How did you know it was a she?"

Margaret shrugged. She wondered whether to mention the woman she had seen, then changed her mind.

"Yes, there was a writer used to stay," Catriona continued slowly, "but not anymore. She, well . . . she's away now."

"Anyone famous?" asked Margaret. "What did she write?"

Catriona seemed to hesitate, and Margaret wondered if perhaps she was inviting a breach of confidentiality. The writer might, very naturally, not wish to be named, to become a subject of gossip.

"Sorry. I didn't mean to be nosy."

"No, no! Not very well known. She wrote under a pseudonym. Hermione Lake. We knew her as Karen. I think her books sold well in America—she was from Boston. She stayed a few times a year. For the peace and tranquillity, she said. Oh, yes. She liked our old tales— Scottish roots, you see."

"She wrote history?"

"No, not really. Scottish historical romance. Stuff to do with legends, that kind of thing."

"You knew her well?"

"Yes and no. She kept to herself, mainly. Used to come round here for a wee dram." Catriona laughed, an attractive peal. "For inspiration. It's the Scottish ancestry. Talking of which . . . maybe you'll join me in a glass?"

"Well, it's a little early," said Margaret, checking her watch, "but, well, I won't say no."

Already Catriona was pouring generous measures from a cut-glass decanter. "Famous Grouse all right?"

Margaret laughed. "Anything."

They sipped and shared eulogies to the lowly brand's unassuming quality. "Fine in moderation," Catriona declared, assuming a solemn face.

"Absolutely," said Margaret, "Er . . . how old was she?"

"How old? Karen? Well, she was only fifty-five when she . . . "

"Why did she leave?"

"Oh, I don't think she was so well . . . Look, I'll see if I've any of her books here." She went to an untidy array of shelves, diligently searching.

"No, sorry, I'll have a look round the house . . . She wrote a children's book too. In her real name. It was about seals—a wee bit macabre. Very good, though. And a little book about legends. Including some from Shuna." She laughed. "Ghosties and ghoulies have a field day up here, you know."

Catriona stood. "Well, we must be getting on," she said with finality. "Aye, there's work to do."

"Whereabouts is the cottage?" insisted Margaret. "The map—it isn't clear? I wondered if I saw it up near the church . . . "

"Aye, that way. By the chapel." MacBeath's voice came from behind. His tone was short. She was unsure how long he had been standing there. He was wafting disapprovingly at the smoke-filled air. A swift glance passed between him and his wife, difficult to read. Did he object to carousing while work awaited?

"It's all shut up now," he added authoritatively. "Nothing to see."

"Oh! Don't forget!" said Catriona, smiling, as Margaret got up. "Your wine! I'll fetch it now. Didn't get a chance to get round."

So it had not been Catriona in the garden? The more she thought about it, the likeness was all wrong anyway.

Margaret hesitated.

"I, er . . . is there anyone else living here? Near here, I mean? Near me? A neighbour maybe? A woman? . . . I thought I saw someone, that's all." She described her, such as she could recall.

Catriona eyed her husband.

"Well, now!" she said hesitantly, "That must be Dorothy. Gordon's lass. I didn't know she was back from school . . . She likes to watch the seals down there."

"Aye, she goes out that way." MacBeath's face was stony.

"Gordon's our factor," Catriona explained. "Dorothy's his daughter. Not quite right in the head, poor lass. Only fifteen. A real shame. An accident, years ago . . . A bit of a fright to look at. But harmless. She was wondrous bonnie as a wee lass. Don't mind her. I'll have a word with Gordon."

Margaret departed less than reassured. The thought of her solitude being disturbed by a headcase was not comforting.

Returning, Margaret found herself on an unfamiliar path. Ahead was a glade of trees, their boles gleaming in a swift pale beam of sunshine. Beyond was the loch. Margaret noticed near the shoreline above thick shrubs the corner of a roof—was this the one she had first glimpsed from the moor and assumed to be her own?

Margaret paused. Was this, then, where Dorothy lived? She wasn't sure she wanted to find out. She retraced her steps, picking up the correct path, hurrying back to her own cottage. Entering the dell, she warily surveyed the scene, walking round the house, going down as far as the shore, then back up the burn. Lethargic seals eyed her curiously from the rocks, then slithered into the sea.

The Chardonnay proved excellent; it was good to know supplies existed, maybe whisky too. Catriona was a true Scot—she need fear no disapproval there. Of her husband, Margaret was not so sure. He hadn't liked their little tipple, or the smoking. A latter-day John Knox, and they the Monstrous Regiment! The evening faded languorously. It was only when she stood up to fix the fire, stumbling in the hearth, that she realised she had drunk too much. She surveyed the whisky with alarm: but there was still some left—the best part of half a bottle, really.

She stepped outside into the cool night air to clear her head, lighting a last cigarette. The moon was almost full, its brilliance exaggerated in the Caledonian night-sky. The stars, too, were vivid, nearer, more multitudinous than in Oxfordshire. The seals were calling again, doleful, outlandish, a macabre threnody. Somewhere a bird, deluded by the moon, was twittering a premature dawn chorus. Margaret meandered to the shore, where the moonbeams traced a shimmering path along the obsidian waters, weaving their rippling tracery like strands of delicate, pale fabric.

Gazing on the eerie scene, listening to the seals, Margaret became aware again of the same uncomfortable sensation as previously, as if she were being watched. It felt all the more alarming in the dark. It was worrying someone should be about, prowling on her patch at so late an hour; it was gone one o'clock. Could it be Dorothy? There was no knowing what a girl like that might be up to. Harmless she might be, but Margaret did not relish encountering her here at this hour of the night.

Quickly she turned and faced the cottage, driven by a sudden certainty. She knew what she had sensed: somebody, or something, had passed between her and the light from the parlour window. Anxiously, she swept her eyes around the moonlit garden. Then another idea gripped her, even worse: what if the occlusion of the light had been caused not by any movement outside, but by a presence within? Had someone gained entry to the cottage while she sauntered by the loch?

Cautiously, she returned, wondering what on earth she would do if she encountered Dorothy. Again, as that morning, the sensation shifted: it was as if it soared over to the rugged, moon-etched slopes of the mainland, then back to Shuna, settling at last in the vicinity of the burn. The bubbling of the waters, as they tumbled to the shore, cut the night's stark silence. For a moment, she imagined a shifting flash of greyness, a dim figure, but it was just the moonbeams dancing on the cataract. The laments of the seals had recommenced. They reminded Margaret of the keening at a funeral she had once attended in the west of Ireland.

The first thing she did, once she had ascertained there was no one in the cottage, was to check the wood-store door. Alarmingly, the bolt was not securely fastened, though she was sure she had locked it tight. She listened at the door, tentatively calling out a hallo. Silence brooded within. Wild horses could not have dragged her inside. Nevertheless, she summoned up the nerve to go outside and check the outer door. She even shone the torch through the small, cobwebbed window. There appeared to be nothing.

Margaret poured herself another whisky. Shaking, she sat down in the parlour and lit a cigarette. And then another horror struck her: she could have sworn that, as soon as twilight fell, she had drawn the curtains shut. Yet there they were, wide open, blackness gaping, a yawning gulf in the night. Unsteadily, she got up and closed them, and treble-checked the wood-store door. Of course, with all the drink, she could have forgotten, become confused— this was getting more and more a problem lately. It was three more cigarettes and another glass before she went unsteadily to bed.

Margaret awoke with the dismaying alertness of a hangover. It was still dark. Her head was pounding, her body ached, her mouth tasted foul. A wild, unfocused anxiety seared her nerves. All she wanted was to sleep, yet this was the one salve denied. Grim thoughts besieged her, racing like frenzied demons through her mind. Despair, like a monstrous raincloud, spread over her. In the blackness of the early morning hours, alone in a strange place, she felt herself slipping into the nethermost pit of misery.

Lying all too conscious in her jangled state, this time there was no mistaking it. This was no dream: a muffled thump, a vibration which made the whole house tremble. Her horror of the wood-store came back. A dreadful notion seized her. What if Dorothy *had* somehow got into it? Had she locked the girl inside? The last thing she felt like doing was going to find out. She listened long and anxiously, but no further sound disturbed the silent hour before the dawn.

The more she thought about it, the more Margaret wondered if the sound she had heard the first night really had been located in the wood-store—that had been merely an assumption based on a hazy dream. And yet the sound, she was sure, was identical. It certainly came from within the house. This time the disturbance had seemed, in truth, to come from up above.

An idea was surfacing in her mind, arising from an idle thought which had come to her last night as she lolled by the fire, staring at the ceiling. There ran across the wood-store an exposed beam, clearly a main support of the building; yet it had no visible counterpart in the living quarters; all the rooms had flat ceilings. The beam must continue in a concealed section of the roof. Was it there, maybe, that the noise originated, in an attic of some kind? But where was the access?

Margaret lay miserable in the hell of hangover until the pale light of dawn crept in, and the birds commenced their cacophony.

The first thing, on arising, was a glass of wine. The hair of the dog was the oldest cliché in the book. Fortunately— or unfortunately—it never failed; at least it smoothed the roughest edges. With a bravado she did not feel, she swung wide the wood-store door. Vacancy yawned, menacing and miserable. She eyed the roof-beam, noting its now obvious invisible continuation above the parlour. Quickly, she gathered up more logs, double-checking she had secured the bolt.

Margaret was contemplating whether she could face breakfast when there came a rap at the front door; in her frayed state, she started. As she wondered about answering it, Catriona's voice pealed out.

Hastily concealing the wine bottle and straightening her hair, she opened the door.

"The milk you ordered. Can't leave it on the step, you know. We don't want the Glaistig thinking it's for her."

"Sorry?" said Margaret, her head pounding, "The Glaistig?"

"Aye! You don't know the old tale? The dairymaid kidnapped by the fairies. Don't laugh about her! Oh, no!"

Catriona put the milk on the floor, then reached into a plastic bag, drawing out two books. "I knew I had them. Karen's books. Borrow them. I thought I had the one about the legends too, but I'm missing it. I'll keep looking."

Margaret examined them with interest. One was a children's story, with illustrations, *Morag and the Seals*. The other, a novel, had a lurid dust cover of a woman on a pyre; it was titled *Confession*.

"Thanks. I could do with some reading."

Catriona appeared to linger.

"Are you sure you're all right here?" she asked. "Not too lonely, or . . . anything? . . . Nothing you need?"

Margaret wondered whether to say anything about last night, but it would sound ridiculous. She was on the point of asking more about Dorothy, but the moment passed. A vehicle's horn blared. Beyond the dell MacBeath loomed grim-faced on his buggy. Briefly he raised his hand.

"Well," said Catriona, glancing over her shoulder, "we're off to Fort William. Don't forget, if there is anything . . . don't hesitate . . . Tomorrow. Come and have a chat. And a wee dram!"

The couple seemed to have some altercation before they drove off. Margaret had the impression Catriona had come to say something more, something she did not wish to speak about in her husband's presence.

After breakfast she browsed the books. *Confession* was based on the true story of Isobel Gowdie, the last witch burnt in Scotland, in 1662. There was a good deal of historical detail and, to judge from the blurb, a grimly romantic plot. It was signed on the title page: Hermione Lake, in bold, melodramatic script. The children's book, however, bore the writer's real name, Karen McTavish, duly signed in a more sober hand: the private and the public personas. This looked worth reading.

The hand-drawn illustrations were by the author; it was possible to recognise scenes on Shuna, including her own cottage, the burn running by, the seals gathered on the rocks. The seals were drawn with a macabre panache. It told the tale of a little girl, Morag, who loved to play with the seals and listen to their melancholy songs; so much so that she came more and more to resemble them and learned their strange tongue. One night she disappeared and was never seen again; though her sad voice could be heard singing, mostly in the dawn, or when the evening shadows grew, especially on nights when the moon was bright. Sometimes her face was seen, peeping from the waters of the loch, curiously watching, pining for the world she had forsaken for the Selkies.

Certainly, Karen McTavish had captured the strangeness, the lonely isle's *genius loci*. The tale was poignant, the writing subtle, musical, infused with the spirit of the Hebrides; the spirit which resonated through all the haunting folk songs, all the ancient legends. It was more than a child's tale; it was a fable of ineffable sorrow, of loss and loneliness, unattainable bliss. In her fragile state, Margaret found herself on the edge of tears. All the sadness, all the faded opportunities, all the joys once held that she had let slide through her hands, not cherishing enough: her life whirled by, ever-receding, like a distant island fading in the haze of evening, a vanishing paradise. To think it had all led to this. Drinking herself stupid, all alone, on a Godforsaken Scottish island. No wonder she was starting to imagine things. It was as if Karen McTavish herself reached out from the pages, sharing with her, a kindred spirit, the phantoms of her own torment.

Margaret embarked on a walk to shake off her maudlin mood. She circuited the island, continuing past Shuna House, beside the jetty, then the length of the southern shore. It was sheltered in the wind's lee, but as she climbed the hill at the island's other end it came whooshing harshly down. Out to sea the skies had a wintry cast; showers were gathering above the isles. Completing the island circuit quicker than expected, she soon found herself on the home stretch, passing the chapel ruins.

Margaret stopped. Somewhere here was Karen McTavish's cottage. She must have passed it by. Looking back, there it was, rising above an emerald mossy ridge beside the sound. It commanded a wide prospect, where the loch widened and joined the sea; on a fine day Skye would be visible.

But *was* it her cottage? It appeared rather large. Margaret approached, confused. The windows and doors were boarded, all shut up—exactly as MacBeath had said. But this place looked as if it had not been inhabited for years. There were signs of creeping dereliction: a thrush flew from a large gap in the roof; ivy obscured the rotting entrance door. Catriona had not said how long ago the writer had departed—somehow, she had imagined it as recent. Margaret pondered. Was this, perhaps, the old school house? A survey of the region revealed no other building, compounding the mystery. Her head thumped. Dissatisfied and depressed, tired by conundrums, she hastened away. In minutes she was back on her own territory, heralded by the tinkling burn.

Margaret froze in her tracks.

There on the path, where the burn rippled over stepping-stones, crouched Dorothy: straggle-haired, gypsy-like, clad in greyish rags, a waif, wild and neglected. She was dabbling in the waters, singing to herself, a kind of demented lullaby.

Luckily, the girl's back was turned. The only way Margaret could think to avoid her was to wind round the shore, crossing the stream lower down, approaching the cottage from the loch side, though she doubted she could stay entirely out of sight. The transit through brambles and over slimy boulders proved fiendish. Progress was slow, especially as she sought to avoid making any noise. Soon the girl was hidden by a hummock, and by the time Margaret reached the cottage had vanished altogether.

Margaret lit the fire as soon as she got in, fixing cheese and biscuits and a generous whisky. *Confession* was not really to her taste. Hermione Lake wrote in a trite populist style, far removed from the poetic, heartfelt tone of Karen McTavish. Soon she was yawning. She put down the book and tipped the rest of the bottle into her glass. When that was finished, she went into the kitchen for another. It was then she noticed a small trapdoor in the kitchen ceiling;

she was surprised she had not seen it before. This must be the access to the attic. She could not quite reach, and returned to the parlour for a chair to stand on; but, facing the hatch, she saw with irritation that it was padlocked. Foiled, she set about hunting for the key; there was a chance it might be in a drawer, or somewhere handy— unless the MacBeaths held it at the house.

Margaret searched to no avail. In a dusty cupboard she disturbed some worn cookery books, which slid to the floor, scattering. As she bent down to retrieve them, she saw that one was not a cook book: it bore Karen McTavish's name on the cover and a picture of a weeping woman. It was a book of Scottish legends—the very one mentioned by Catriona, a large illustrated paperback. The author's neat signature was inside.

Margaret browsed at random. Each chapter covered a separate legend. She recognised the Glaistig, mentioned by Catriona. The legends were recounted in compelling prose, with remarkably plausible line-drawings, some of them quite unnerving, as if witnessed at first hand: the Urisk, the Kelpie, the Brownie, the Beannighe, the Luideag. Here was the same picture of the Selkies as in *Morag and the Seals*.

A small, stained sheet of paper slipped from the rear fold of the dustjacket. It was written, by the look of it, with a fountain pen in dark blue ink. It was in Karen's own hand. The ink had run in parts; not all of it was legible . . .

It was a form of personal confession, agonised, sorrowful, tragic. It spoke of malady and madness, the pain of an affliction Margaret knew, oh so well, herself. Certain passages were underscored in red ink. Once more, Margaret felt that she gazed into the anguished soul of Karen McTavish . . .

Daily now, my strength fails. I can no longer work or even think straight. I watch the seals, yearning like Morag for their ineffable serenity. Languid they lie upon the restless shore, all-seeing, all-knowing. I hear their twilight wails of mourning. They mourn, alas, for me. No longer can I dream my dreams, nor weave my words, I who once wove tapestries of moonbeams. I am dying inch by inch.

A last paragraph, untidily written in a different shade of ink, appeared to have been added later, in trembling haste:

My time, I know, cannot now be long. These several days and nights, here on my very threshold, I have beheld her, readying my funeral shroud. She who washes at the ford. Tonight I shall go willingly, be it by my own shaking hand . . .

Margaret's attention shifted back to the attic. Its presence brooded uneasily on her mind.

She stepped back on the chair and fiddled frantically with the padlock. Amazingly it slipped open and fell clattering to the floor. Torch in hand, she swept the gloom and peered within. Here too was a smell of patchouli. She could see the timber beam extending over the parlour, through to the wood-store, just as predicted. Shredded cardboard boxes lay around, a scene of rodent depredation. Squirrels? Could they have caused the noise? One box was torn wide open, gnawed to its base. From it strewed ravaged garments: a green velvet shawl; the ragged remnants of a stripy satin blouse; tattered Indian headscarves; a fur coat in holes; a chic, red-leather, hipster jacket, stained with mildew. The detritus of an arty female's wardrobe.

Margaret closed the trapdoor pensively. An unwelcome thought was gestating in her mind . . .

In moments she had fled the house, stumbling through the dell, hurrying along the track to the jetty. Taking the deviation she had wandered into earlier, she reached the glade; the naked trees glistened in the dying twilight. This time she proceeded further up as far as the cottage—what remained of it.

It had been destroyed by fire. Bare, scorched branches crowded round like twisted claws. This was not Dorothy's cottage, nor any worker's cottage. It was the one MacBeath had twice let slip: burnt down by a careless guest, gone to ruin. These trees—surely they were rowans?

Margaret's head reeled.

This was Rowan Cottage—the confusion of the maps suddenly made shocking sense. *The cottage she had been looking for—no wonder she had been unable to find it— it was the one she was staying in, the one in which Karen McTavish had* . . .

A slow panic possessed her. Clearly, the MacBeaths had not wanted her to know the truth: Catriona's guilty solicitude, her husband's prevarications—it all fitted. Clearly they had not wished to tell her because Karen's departure had partaken of the sinister. There was something they wanted to hide. And MacBeath had tried to mislead her, lying to her, implying Karen's cottage was the derelict schoolhouse. Margaret recalled the looks that passed between them, the reticence, the evasions. And Catriona's hesitation.

She was only fifty-five when she . . .

Intuition dawned . . .

She had felt uneasy ever since her arrival . . . the dwelling was unquiet, possessed . . . the things she had heard, sensed, imagined, glimpsed on the edge of sight . . . the feeling of being watched . . . the strange thoughts, the sorrow, the harrowing despair . . .

The noises in the attic and the wood-store were one and the same. Whatever had happened in the wood-store had vibrated in the roof, that was all; it had not been just a sound, she had felt it like a force. The shaking of the beam, the beam than ran the full length of the house, jolting when something heavy fell from it, when Karen McTavish, in drink-saturated misery, had hanged herself.

Margaret stood paralysed, perplexed, as twilight's embers faded. The moon was waxing, improbably huge like an alien planet, bathing the lonely scene in a wan, ghostly radiance, chasing shifting shadows. A chill breeze blew off the loch. The prospect of spending another night in the cottage, within its anguished walls, was mortifying. No more could she face the wood-store with its littered bottles, or sleep beneath the attic with its melancholy glad-rags.

She rushed to Shuna House; she must speak to Catriona. Yet what was she to say? That she was haunted by Karen's ghost? That she knew she had hanged herself in the cottage? That they had been lying to her? It was, after all, on sober reckoning, only supposition. MacBeath would put it down to drink, she had caught his disapproving looks. But Catriona knew—she bore within her soul the sensibility, the insight of the Hebrides. *Are you sure you're all right here?*

Margaret knocked repeatedly and loudly, but the sole response was Charlie's furious barking. No lights were on, nor was there smoke from the chimney. They must still be at Fort William. Night was almost upon her. All the time it was getting colder, the penetrating chill of a Scottish April. The only thing was to brave it out one more night.

Wine and whisky would see her through, they always did, sweet waters of oblivion.

The dell was dim in rhododendron shadows, the cottage a silent presence. Garden and loch were swathed in pale moonlight. She could hear the seals crying; almost, she imagined, she could make out words, a litany of inconsolable grief. Never had their voices sounded so achingly beautiful— yet so eloquent of desolation. Margaret felt enticed, drawn towards the rippling dark waters of the loch.

It was then that she heard another sound, an eerie counterpoint to the seals, a low, soft crooning.

Too late she saw who it was, chanting to herself in the tumbling burn—the hunched shoulders, the raggedy clothes, the straggly black locks. The last thing she needed. Margaret paused, retreating silently, but her nervous feet dislodged a stone. It rolled, splashing loudly in the burn.

Dorothy turned around.

A bit of a fright to look at but harmless.

Catriona's words came back. But fifteen years old? This creature looked a hundred. Or was it a wasted fifty-five?

Margaret recoiled, seized with mortal dread. The wizened crone simply stared and smiled, singing her sad harmonies, persisting with her task, pounding in the running water with a large flat stone, washing a voluminous white garment.

Margaret cried out, stumbled, lost her balance, sliding on the wet grass. She fell into the burn's declivity, where the rocks were sharp and lethal. The seals wailed out their paeans of mourning.

※

The MacBeaths waited at the jetty as the police launch plied its way towards them through the frothing waters.

Catriona stubbed out her cigarette. "They're not going to like this. Two fatalities in the space of nine months. It was bad enough last time."

"Two clear cases. Suicide and accident, these things happen."

"Aye, I suppose so. But I told you, no one should have been put in that place. It has a bad feel, always has had—even before Karen came."

"You and your Tobermory superstitions! Don't be talking that nonsense to the police! Where else could we have put her? We've still got no electricity in the others. We need the money, you know that."

"Aye. But, you know, she was troubled, I could tell. That cottage. It's unquiet. Charlie won't go near the place. It scares me, you know that."

"Rubbish! Look, she was an alcoholic too. You should've seen what was in those bags. I had to lift them! That's the only spirit that was haunting her. You can imagine anything in that state. Look how paranoid she got about Dorothy."

The launch was pulling alongside. Two officers were stepping out onto the jetty. They were not smiling.

"Aye!" said Catriona, lighting another cigarette, "Now that's a funny thing. Did I not tell you?"

"What?" snapped MacBeath.

"I saw Gordon yesterday and asked him about Dorothy."

"So?"

"Well, Dorothy's still away."

Inheritance

As the train snaked into the dark heart of the city, Isobel fell to wondering why it was that railway lines everywhere seemed to pass through undiscovered country. A country of the mind as much as anything material.

Whether past drab suburban housing sprawls, deserted factories or the towering columns of city buildings, she could never quite relate the places she was seeing to conventional reality. It was as if the engineers had carved their iron highway through lost dimensions, zones denied to inhabitants of the outside world. Here in the subterranean canyons of a vast foreign metropolis, as the train trundled the final mile towards the terminus, she experienced a feeling close to panic. But, then, Isobel was never a comfortable traveller.

In fact, it would be no exaggeration to say Isobel cherished a positive loathing for travel. It was a foible that, if truth be told, had brought about the end of her only relationship; and with it any prospect of insurance against the loneliness that swirled around her like a void. This short trip away, to a small town in Germany, was proving, absurdly, to be a daunting experience; a nameless foreboding stalked her relentlessly. Yet it was one trip she really felt she ought to make.

Martje she had met the previous summer on a tour of Scotland, the kind of holiday that Isobel could handle, where everything was arranged, courier-chaperoned, in sumptuous luxury. Like herself, just past the dread frontier of fifty, and with a vague history of a failed love affair, Martje had proved a kindred spirit, an extrovert to counter Isobel's introversion. There was a good deal of shared resignation at the vicissitudes of life. It was that kind of bond.

Isobel was making the journey in belated response to her friend's repeated invitations, to visit her at her home in Dorf, not far from the Dutch border. It was a cold, damp February, not the best time of year to travel. Like much in life, it had seemed a good idea at the time; now she was not so sure.

The train was slowing to a halt, waiting interminably, the rapid German words explaining the delay menacing, incomprehensible. They had entered a dark tunnel-like cutting. Through the windows Isobel could see only grimy walls. At intervals the darkness was relieved by electric lamps, palely gleaming from the walls like rheumy eyes. She peered out into the Stygian gloom: a spindly plant struggled up from a crack in the dripping stone, lankly reaching for the distant sky. Only a narrow gap separated them from the wall. Her own reflection stared back at her, unflattering and pallid.

It was as the train began to move again, like a reluctant beast goaded into languid motion, that Isobel saw the doll.

At least she thought it was a doll: the size of an infant—though it was hard to be sure in the muted light. It was leaning against the wall, arms awry, stumpy legs stretched towards the track. Its old fashioned clothes were torn and filthy, its face battered, its discoloured, patchy hair askew, like an ill-fitting wig. Hurled down to its doom, no doubt, by some disgruntled child from the heights above, it looked like the victim of a grim accident. In wild parody, a beatific smile wreathed its blotchy features. Isobel gazed through the glimmering haze, but the vision passed in the flicker of an instant, as, finally, the train sidled its way into the maw of the terminus.

Cologne station felt huger and more confusing than any she had previously known, with its multitude of platforms, its immense echoing noise. Checking her watch against the platform clock, she saw she had forty minutes before her connection. Isobel was relieved to discover her train would depart from the same platform, necessitating no negotiation of the subway labyrinth or braving the bellowing of the concourse. There was even a cafeteria where she could while away the time without appearing to be lingering.

Replenished by coffee, amulet against the wilderness, Isobel looked forward to seeing Martje again. She felt excited and restless, like an adolescent. There would be lots to chat about, highlights of their holiday, secrets to confide.

But even as she contemplated the pleasing prospect of reunion, Isobel could not rid her mind of the hideous doll. Sipping the strong continental coffee, she longed for the stimulus of the cigarettes she had given up three months ago. She did not feel any better for it, and they had been an old reliable ally in the perpetual battle against the demons of anxiety. The horrid vision had rekindled a fervently repressed childhood memory.

It concerned the terrible events surrounding the demise, some four decades ago, of her sister, Lucy . . .

Isobel was only six when Lucy arrived; she was, in reality, her step-sister, an adopted orphan. Lucy's arrival as a fully formed playmate, about three years of age, and not as a mewling babe, was no disadvantage to Isobel, who was only too pleased to welcome to her world a new companion. There were hints of a tragedy that had befallen Lucy's family, its precise nature never revealed by Isobel's father (her own mother had died when the girls were still young children). There was some suggestion Lucy was of foreign ancestry; certainly, Isobel had memories of the strange-sounding words with which the three year old had at first articulated her frustrated demands.

There was no obvious connection between the beautiful, blue-eyed doll Lucy brought with her from her mysterious past and the harrowing circumstances culminating in her dramatic self-destruction. Isobel, however, loathed the doll from the day it entered the household; coming in later years to regard it as harbinger of disaster. Her parents at first treated Isobel's revulsion as a form of displaced jealousy, scolding her, cajoling her, but eventually respecting this mystifying quirk. Isobel had never been able to explain, even to herself, precisely why the doll frightened her so much.

But frighten her it most certainly did. There were times when Isobel could hardly bear to run the gauntlet of its human gaze, hear its bleating baby voice; or touch the quaint garments that Lucy so enjoyed rearranging, the thick red hair she never tired of combing. For she adored the doll with a passion greater than she displayed towards any other toy; even greater, Isobel suspected, than towards her adoptive parents. Lucy always called her doll Katrina, though nobody ever knew the provenance of the name. Certainly it was ancient. A farewell gift, perhaps, given her for her journey to a new life in a foreign land, far away from home?

Maybe it was just the doll's antiquity, dimly sensed by the six-year-old Isobel that made it so uncanny. Or its disquietingly lifelike look. Or was it to do with the fact that it was so exquisitely made, a work of subtle craft, an adult artefact rather than a child's toy? Indeed, it was a miracle such a fragile object should have survived childhood's depredations—though, it had to be admitted, Lucy always treated her beloved doll with an astonishingly meticulous respect.

During sleepless nights, Isobel wanted to get up while the house was silent, go downstairs and smash the hateful thing to smithereens, to consign it forever to oblivion; but, quite apart from the practical objections, she was simply too afraid. Eventually a compromise had been reached, whereby the irksome doll remained confined to Lucy's own bedroom, which across a space of years, Isobel never dared to enter. Sometimes in the silence of the night she imagined she could hear the two inseparable companions murmuring and muttering, conversing with each other in an unintelligible tongue.

Lucy's obsession with Katrina had probably been an early warning sign of the illness, the madness that, by her early teens, would possess her; banishing her to that forbidding "home" where tragedy would pile on tragedy. Isobel shuddered at the memories she had tried so constantly to suppress but here, in an alien land, in the bleak anonymity of the echoing railway station, terror came flooding back.

Her father, ultimately, had faced little choice; the doctors' meddling, as so often happens, only making matters worse. Lucy was confined to an institution run by nuns, a grim Victorian building in the trash-strewn no man's land of inner city Liverpool. Katrina, to Isobel's unspeakable relief, departed with her . . .

There were still nineteen minutes to wait for her train, and her coffee had gone cold. Ordering another, she searched instinctively in her bag for the non-existent cigarettes she no longer smoked, cursing silently . . .

It was perhaps unfair to hold the Holy Sisters of Redemption responsible for the subsequent catastrophe; though certainly they were criticised for complacency tantamount to negligence. For it came about, a few months following her incarceration in the House of the Blessed Virgin, that the fourteen year old Lucy was found to be with child. Whilst abortion might have been judged the most charitable course of action, religious considerations dictated otherwise; and Lucy was made to bear her child, which in cruel parody of her own fate was sent away into adoption. Isobel never found out where.

Two years later, in the raw early hours of a February morn, Lucy threw herself from a third floor window. The seventeen-year old Isobel was called to identify the corpse, forlorn amidst the rubbish in the freezing gloom of dawn. Lucy was lying at the foot of the institution's smoke-grimed walls, soaring up behind like a cliff face.

What was so disturbing about the doll she had just seen was that it had reminded her of Lucy's broken body, lying in the debris.

As to the fate of Lucy's doll, Isobel knew nothing. At the time, the larger tragedy prevailed. It was certainly not a thing she was keen to retrieve. It was not among her step-sister's effects, and the nuns feigned incomprehension. Possibly they had destroyed it, unhealthy and idolatrous object; or shuffled it away with the baby. Or maybe Lucy had leaped, her grotesque companion in her arms, into the final abyss.

They were, after all, inseparable . . .

Immersed in her morbid thoughts, Isobel only just caught her connection. The automatic doors snapped shut, impatient and peremptory, seconds after she bustled aboard; already, before she had even found a seat, the train was gathering pace.

Martje, to her relief, was just the same. She hugged Isobel and kissed her on the cheek in continental fashion, lingering just a second longer than formality required. Her breath reeked of the wine and cigarettes on which she thrived. Immediately they slipped back into familiarity, taking up conversation as if it were only yesterday they had spoken; as if they had known each other all their lives. Brandishing a packet of Marlboro, Martje lit up a cigarette, inhaling deeply.

"Given up, Isobel?" she exclaimed. "You have not, I hope, given up alcohol?" She laughed. "In my house I have plenty. We will take a taxi? Already I have had too much to drink to bring my car."

"A drink's just what I *do* need, Martje!" Isobel declared. A flicker of concern in Martje's eyes gave her the eerie feeling that she had read her mind, sensed her recent shock. Should she tell her about it? *Such a weird thing I saw! You'll probably laugh!* Isobel steered away, proceeding to an absurdly upbeat account of her journey. Could it really be herself she heard, enthusing so animatedly about the scary fun of flying?

Martje, though somewhat the older of the two, looked younger. In contrast to the greying streaks advancing through her own black hair, her friend looked scarcely more than forty; she had thick blonde locks clipped page-boy style. Was it a scintilla of envy that made her think the tight-fitting leather trouser suit Martje wore so elegantly was too young for her? So different from her own sober tweeds. Certainly, even if her figure had allowed, Isobel would not have been seen dead in an outfit like that.

As the beige Mercedes taxi raced them home, Martje chattered incessantly. Her command of English was fluent, and strangely attractive with its strongly accented words and frequent lapses into not-quite-accurate idiom; though tainted with that curious transatlantic inflexion, whereby statements are uttered in the form of a question. Occasionally, she intruded words of German, as if the speed of her talk ran ahead of her control. Endless cigarettes had honed her voice into a sexy harshness, exaggerated when she laughed, which she did a lot. Isobel felt she could keep listening forever.

Martje earned a living as an antique dealer, which sounded much more exciting than Isobel's job as a librarian. She had taken over the business from her father, who had died ten years previously. An only child, she had inherited the family home, a substantial nineteenth century residence on the edge of town.

In almost no time at all, the taxi drew up outside the gates of an elegant white house, screened from the road by a straggling laurel hedge and looming pines. A straight suburban street, tree-lined, with modern houses and apartments, extended in both directions, parallel lines stretching to infinity. Dorf looked unremarkable: the kind of place partisans battled over in World War II movies, or the location of a safe house in a story by John Le Carré.

As she paid the taxi, Martje lit up another cigarette from the pack she had been grasping throughout the journey.

A log fire was soon blazing in the spacious fireplace of Martje's comfortable drawing room. Gilt-framed oil paintings, vague in the shimmering half-light, looked down upon them. Flames danced from silver candelabra. A Beethoven sonata was playing quietly in the background.

Tall windows, curtains not yet drawn, stared out into the February night, gilding the feeling of cosiness within. Isobel, now she was ensconced within the womb of security, an expectant glass in her hand, felt her anxieties melting.

"Krug champagne, only the best," Martje announced, placing a silver tray upon a deal table near the fire. "I am saving this for you coming? And then we are having with the meal Chateauneuf du Pape? Only the best." Popping the cork, she poured the fizzling golden nectar into crystal glasses and raised a toast: "*Prost!*"

"Cheers! Here's to kindred spirits," responded Isobel. They clinked glasses.

"Kindred spirits," affirmed Martje. "This house," she continued, "was built in 1895. It has always belonged to my family. Since my father died, I have lived here alone. Before that, I lived in Köln. I was married, in fact . . . " She made a dismissive gesture, then laughed. "But that, as you say in England, is another story."

Soon the two companions, inebriated and voluble, were dining at Martje's lavish table. The flickering candlelight was sparkling through the wine glasses in all the colours of the spectrum. As Isobel, suddenly realising how hungry she was, gratefully devoured her meal, she was happy for her friend to dominate the conversation, the stridency of Martje's voice and the curiosity of her idioms increasing in proportion to the quantity of alcohol imbibed. The wine was going quickly to her head; she would probably get a hangover.

Over coffee and liqueurs, conversation shifted from the trivial to the serious; it was the time for confidences. Isobel could barely recognise her own selective autobiography; whilst Martje's tale, for all her drama and hyperbole, proved an all too mundane tragedy of infidelity and marooning on the rocks of loneliness; though both, with boisterous clashing of the priceless glasses, agreed that now they would not have it otherwise. Only with great willpower did Isobel keep refusing the endlessly proffered cigarettes. Should she confide in Martje about the doll? Even the whole farrago of her morbid history? But the wine, which moments before was releasing her from inhibitions, was now making it difficult to think straight. The moment passed.

The following morning was surprisingly fine for February, but spoilt for Isobel by a vicious hangover. She had suffered a restless night, plagued by hazily recalled nightmares, their mood of dread and dimly fig-ured horrors lingering. The previous evening's euphoria had given way to dejection, and she had a vague idea she had talked a lot of nonsense. She almost felt embarrassed to confront her companion of last night. In the cold light of day, she was glad she had shied away from the matter of the doll, not to speak of more intimate confessions, which now seemed as incommunicable as they were macabre.

Martje, who had been up since six, was busy repairing upholstery on a *chaise longue*. She was, evidently, one of those people who can consume vast quantities of drink and wake the following day feeling all right. A cigarette smouldered in a heaped ashtray. The welcome aroma of fresh ground coffee suffused the room. Isobel gratefully accepted a cup. They sat at the window, beyond which extended a large wooded garden. The winter sunshine glinting brightly on the laurel leaves, only served to edge Isobel's headache with further daggers. She refused any breakfast. Martje was outlining the day's arrangements.

"First, Isobel," she said, "I will show you round, and show you my antiques? They are in all the rooms. Many I inherited. But some I bought by myself. Unfortunately, I have to go out to see a client. You'll be okay here? Get rid of that hangover."

Wracked by nausea, Isobel trailed behind her hostess, exploring the spacious house. On three floors, it was still of a size comfortably manageable for someone living on their own, especially one who knew, like Martje, how to fill the space with *objets d'art*. It made Isobel think of a stately home in miniature. Though her acquaintance with old valuables went no further than the *Antiques Roadshow*, she admired the treasures cluttering the rooms and corridors, about which her friend waxed volubly and knowingly.

Martje's especial pride was her collection of antique mirrors, displayed in bewildering variety: in polished wood, or in elaborately patterned metalwork; others wholly glass, embossed or plain, in every shape and dimension. Not all were perfect in reflection, but it was an education in a dying art that so many were that much truer than those generally for sale in a modern department store. Isobel, disconcertingly, kept confronting multiple images of herself; a phenomenon, she supposed, more palatable to her attractive companion. The endlessly replicating panorama, through doorways and corridors, over stairwells and landings, created an air of the surreal, confusing size and space, distorting angles of perception, opening up vortices of terrifying, infinite regression.

It was within this mirrored labyrinth that Isobel glimpsed the doll.

The apparition, multiplied a dozen times, sprang across her consciousness for a fraction of a second, a subliminal image, as they traversed the third floor landing. At first Isobel wondered if she were experienc-ing a hallucination, a malfunction of the brain spawned by the night's excesses.

Martje, buoyed up by her own enthusiasm, was oblivious to her friend's dismay. Or perhaps it was just that her petrified expression, her growing pallor, beaming back relentlessly from the multitude of mirrors, looked merely symptomatic of a hangover.

Martje was leading her into a room at the rear, overlooking the tall pines of the garden. It was full of toys.

"This, Isobel, used to be my bedroom as a girl."

Martje's impassioned chatter, as she pointed out the antiquity and artistry of the assembled childhood treasures, passed over Isobel. Her eyes were fixed upon a trio of dolls, perched like infants against the back of a settee. Two were of little consequence, a kind that could be bought anywhere. But the doll sitting in the middle, beautiful and blue-eyed, could have been the twin of Katrina. In only one respect did the loathsome figure differ: this doll's hair, as thick and lifelike as her doppelgänger's, was of a rich tawny blonde. The piercing eyes, almost human, stared at her. The blood red lips sketched a grotesque smile. The horrid little limbs seemed to writhe and wriggle, shifting in the old-fashioned garments. The hateful bleating of Katrina's voice, echoing down the years, elicited in Isobel's pounding head an answering cry.

Martje caught her as she reeled.

"Hey! What's up?" she said, as Isobel came to. "Too much champagne! You okay? Perhaps you lie down for a while?"

Isobel's mind was in confusion; there was one question she just had to ask. She tried to mask the quaver in her voice, affecting a casual tone. "The doll," she said, pointing towards the settee, "the one in the middle, the blonde, where did that one come from?"

"Well," responded Martje, hesitating, "she . . . she is a great antique. She is in the family a long time? The other two I got as birthday presents when I was little. Just fifties memorabilia, they are not valuable . . . But Julianna, well, I suppose she is not really a toy? Though she arrived as one, I understand."

Martje paused, as if wondering whether to say more, her tone then stiffening to one of professional aplomb. "Julianna, I am certain, is a genuine Heubach-Köppelsdorf. Leipzig. Circa 1893, I think. They do not make dolls like this anymore . . . Julianna belonged to my cousin, Natassja."

Isobel would not hear of Martje cancelling her client, protesting that coffee, ibruprofen and a rest would cure her. When Martje left the house, she went back upstairs to the bathroom and retched. She noticed with relief that the door to Julianna's room was firmly shut. The murmuring she thought she heard could only be inside her aching head. Rather than retire to her own bed-room—next door to the hateful Julianna—she returned to the drawing room, collapsing onto the *chaise longue*. She fell swiftly into an uncomfortable doze, through which horrors stalked incessantly . . .

Isobel dreamed she was lost in a labyrinthine mansion, where the corridors were flanked with mirrors. It was impossible to decide what was real, what was reflection; on which side of the looking-glass she was imprisoned.

She had a mission to perform . . .

Martje's voice reached her from across an abyss; slowly her surroundings recomposed, it was like regaining consciousness after an anaesthetic. She was lying on the floor by an open window, which wafted in chilly gusts of air. She was in Julianna's room. She had no memory of having got there. Martje was plying her with brandy. The two birthday present dolls stared impassively across the curiously disordered room.

But of Julianna there was not a sign.

Isobel confronted a scene of bizarre disarray. Scattered across the immaculately polished floorboards were hundreds of shards of ceramic or some such substance, mixed with tattered remnants of fine linen. A fire-iron from the drawing room lay amidst the mayhem. A tiny, blonde, dishevelled wig, attached to a sliver of forehead, rested in a distant corner. Two blue eyeballs gazed fixedly up at her from amidst the ruination.

"You are lucky," said Martje. "You were nearly falling out of the window. I just caught you. You were, maybe, feeling sick?"

Martje lit up a Marlboro and made an eloquent gesture round the room.

"Do not worry," she sighed, empathising with Isobel's dismay, "I have sometimes thought of doing the same myself . . . Julianna—what is the expression? She . . . *she gave me the creeps*. So lovely, but . . . *unheimlich*."

Isobel was as stunned at Martje's peculiar composure as she was appalled at her own extravagant vandalism.

"Could you not have sold her?" she asked. "I mean, if you were . . . afraid of her?"

"I could not let her go," said Martje. "She has been in the family a long time. The past, it is so important to me now with so much gone? Aunt Eva, I was very fond of her, and she asked me to keep the doll when she was dying. It was to her like a memento of Natassja? . . . And, I have to confess, there was always the consideration she was a very valuable antique. *Unschätzbar*! Priceless!"

Martje looked remarkably composed for one surveying many thousands of Euro reduced to smithereens.

"Who knows what Julianna would have fetched on the market? The doll is impossibly rare! I did not tell anyone in the trade what I believed I had acquired. It is known, you see, a tiny few were custom made by Heubach-Köppelsdorf, to special order. Nobody I know has ever seen one, or even heard of one for sale!"

She looked Isobel in the eye. "This, I am sure, was one of them. You saw with your own eyes the craft-work."

Martje paused, lighting a fresh cigarette from the glowing stub of its predecessor. Isobel sensed there was more to come, some intimate secret. The presentiment of doom possessing her since the plane had left the runway at Heathrow, hovered like vast wings over the devastated room. Martje's hand was trembling slightly, her eyes glistening.

"My cousin, Natassja," proceeded Martje with regained composure, "died when she was very young. A tragedy—actually, a suicide. She was growing up with my aunt in the 1930s in Dresden, in the East. These were bad times for Germany. You would think, to hear the news every day, it was only the Jews who suffered. But many other Germans were persecuted too. And everyone, if you weren't of the Party, lived in fear. And there was poverty for many, after the inflation and then the depression. My uncle, he died young. My aunt brought Natassja up on her own. There was little money. And, then, in the War, things were even worse, with bombs and starvation. And after that the Russians came."

She paused, pouring herself another drink, replenishing Isobel's glass with the last dregs of Rémy-Martin.

"Growing up in the sixties after my own mother died, Aunt Eva was like a mother to me . . . She confided to me things about Natassja that I know she did not tell anybody else? . . . You see, Natassja was raped by Russian soldiers . . . and she had a child, a girl. It was in the early fifties, before the Wall, and somehow they managed to escape to the West. Then they were living in Düsseldorf. And my cousin, well, she went crazy. They had to put her away in a hospital. My aunt, she was left caring for the little one on her own.

"One winter night, no-one ever knew what really happened, Natassja got out of the awful place and wandered the streets, and somehow she climbed on a parapet and jumped down into one of those tunnels on the railway."

The coldness that swept over Isobel did not come from the open window. She could scarcely take in Martje's continuing tale.

"Of course, I have to say, Natassja was not right in the head for a long time before then. You see, Natassja's own mother, I think, she committed suicide too. It was, what is the phrase? . . . Running in the family?"

"Natassja's *mother*?" said Isobel, mystified, "Eva, your aunt? *She* killed herself? I don't quite follow . . . ?"

"Sorry, did I not say? Natassja was not really my cousin, she was not my aunt's *real daughter*. Natassja was adopted. From a family in Leipzig. My aunt never spoke of the circumstance, except to say there was a tragedy . . . and, well, I worked it out for myself?"

"Who *were* her family, then?"

It was as if Martje's eyes scanned the troubled past.

"Her real family?" she replied pensively. "I do not know. They must have been very rich to have afforded those dolls Natassja brought with her. To have them custom made, even then, would have cost a small fortune. Who knows what was the family's past? There was so much destroyed in the War."

"Dolls, *plural*?" queried Isobel, perplexed. "I don't understand."

Martje returned her gaze.

"Julianna, you see, had a sister, a twin. The only difference was that the other was a redhead. Once, my aunt told me the other one's name, but I have forgotten."

"But, Martje," insisted Isobel, "what *happened* to that doll?"

Martje shrugged. "*Das kann ich mir nicht erklären.* I do not recall. I only heard tell of her, I never saw her. What I know, I got from my aunt, and this was nearly forty years ago. She may have told me, but I don't remember. All I ever had was Julianna."

"And the child, Natassja's baby? What happened to *her*? Are you still in touch? She must be round your age?"

Martje looked nonplussed. "No," she answered, "I never knew her. Did I not say? This was all before my mother died, before I went to live with my aunt? My aunt wished to keep the baby, but she was not so young. She had to put her into care in the end . . . It is cruel that the fate of the daughter and the fate of the mother . . . the madness . . . it was the same? It is like a curse?"

Isobel's mind was racing, intuition overtaking reason.

"Martje," she implored, "where did Natassja's baby go?"

"In the end? I do not know. The child went first to a religious charity in Essen, some kind of orphanage. After that, who knows? . . . Years later there was a big scandal, for the charity was involved in abuse and even trading in children? It was a good thing my aunt was by then dead, it would have broke her heart. The tales cannot be described. I did make enquiries at the time, but there was not a record of Katrina."

"*Katrina?*" Isobel stared, aghast, "*Katrina* was the little girl's name?"

Martje raised both hands to her face. "*Grosse Gott!*" she exclaimed. "*Nein! Nein!* All these years and now I remember. Julianna's twin. Yes, of course, *her name* was Katrina . . . Natassja's baby, no, no, she was called Lucia."

Isobel's mind was slipping back, as through a time warp, to the dark vacancy of no man's land one cold February more than three decades ago, praying she could recollect that somewhere amidst the rubble she had perhaps glimpsed a pair of blue eyeballs staring up at her or a tiny, red, dishevelled wig, attached to a sliver of forehead.

And she was thinking of an unnamed baby that had gone forth into the world, unaccompanied, please, God, from the House of the Blessed Virgin.

This time, when Martje lit another cigarette, automatically brandishing her pack, Isobel took one. Three months down the drain. But she needed this. As Martje leant over with her flaming Ronson, steadying Isobel's trembling wrist, it felt like a sacrament.

A Midsummer Ramble
in the Carpathians

*"We are in Transylvania; and Transylvania is not
England. Our ways are not your ways, and there shall
be to you many strange things."*
> – *Bram Stoker,* Dracula

Julia P. Flint, dealer in antiquarian books and maps,
specialist in topography and travel, could scarcely
believe what she had acquired at the Leyburn book
auction.

Unless she was very much mistaken, what she held
in her hands was the manuscript of an unpublished
journal by no less than Amelia B. Edwards, the renowned
Victorian travel writer, whose accounts of unexplored
lands were amongst the best in the genre. Not so long
ago she had sold a worn first edition with severe spine-
lean and much foxing of *A Thousand Miles up the Nile*
for a three figure sum; she could have sold it ten times
over. This, however, was more akin to her other classic,
Untrodden Peaks and Unfrequented Valleys, concerning
her 1872 expedition to the Dolomites. The journal,
written in pencil, was untitled, undated, unsigned and
incomplete, in a quarto-sized notebook lacking the later
pages. It was a record of a journey through the Southern
Carpathians.

Julia had checked the manuscript innumerable times and could not understand how its provenance had escaped the eyes of the valuers. In the same lot she had acquired rare editions of Freya Stark and a batch of highly collectable books on polar exploration. She had hardly spared a glance at the item's description in the catalogue: "Private journal. Handwritten. Travelogue. Carpathian Mountains. No date. Incomplete. Overall condition Good." The entire lot came from the library of a large house in East Yorkshire. There had been few bids; most of the clients that day had been straight literature collectors, and her acquisition was the sole travel-writing lot. The few half-hearted hands had soon lapsed, and Julia heard the hammer go down at £950. The polar books alone would recoup that.

Several weeks passed before Julia examined the manuscript. She had considered it merely curious dross, the kind of peripheral stuff that turned up in the trade. Stark's tomes had remained stubbornly on the shelves; but a book on the Franklin Expedition had cleared £1000 within a day of appearing in her catalogue. Buoyed up by the news—it would help fend off the bank—Julia, one leisurely Sunday, perused the other items in the lot, beginning with the manuscript. It was quite well-written, indeed excellent. It was not long before an uneasy sense of excitement possessed her.

There is something about literary style, a quality scarcely definable, that to the discerning reader is recognised intuitively: Julia had read this writer before. The anonymous scribe's account was characterised by witty anecdotes about local life, brilliant perorations on art and architecture and, most notably, a vivid evocation of the mountainous landscape. The writer referred constantly to a companion named Lucy . . .

Julia's mind whirled . . .

Lucy? . . . Lucy Renshawe? Amelia B. Edwards's companion on her expedition to the Dolomites— immortalised solely by the letter "L" to conceal from stern Victorian publishers the fact that such bold adventures had been undertaken by a member of the weaker sex unaccompanied.

Julia reached for *A Midsummer Ramble in the Dolomites*, the retitled second edition of *Untrodden Peaks and Unfrequented Valleys*. The more she read, the more she was sure she recognised Edwards's style: witty, ironic, erudite; the nuance of the prose, turns of phrase, word usage, even punctuation, corresponded. Locating a folio edition of her book on Egypt, she compared the manuscript with a photograph of a letter Edwards had written to the British Museum. There could be no doubt—the spacing of the words, the forming of the letters, even the dotting of the "i"s and crossing of the "t"s—this was undoubtedly the hand of Amelia B. Edwards.

Julia wondered about the date. There was no record, so far as she knew, of Edwards ever having visited the Carpathians. The journal was contemporaneous with the events described, set out in the form of an irregularly updated diary in which numerous days, even weeks, were summarised in a single entry. Annoyingly, although the entries were identified between June and October, they cited no year.

If the date was frustrating, more so was the notebook's incompleteness. Half the pages were missing, torn out by the look of it, the text cut out midstream at the end of the last page. Whether deliberate on the author's part, or done by a later custodian, was impossible to say; it could even be natural disintegration. It would reduce its value, but perhaps not that much—things sold in the trade for sums that beggared even Julia's catholic sense of proportion. That Edwards had never sought to publish, or even mention, her Carpathian trip—despite the lure of eulogy and remuneration—was odd; it argued for conscious reticence on her part regarding the whole expedition.

Julia returned to the beginning and read more carefully. It was compelling . . .

❊

The two women, accompanied by Lucy's maid, Sibyl, began their trek at Budapest in mid-June. Edwards brought to her brief description of the city's magnificent skyline in the pink-flecked dawn that sense of the numinous familiar from her travel books. The journal glossed quickly over their passage through Hungary, a relay of stagecoaches, by way of Szolnok and Oradea. From Beiuş they travelled alongside the Black Koros River, passing through the Bihar and Apuseni Mountains and on to Nagy-Szeben— or Sibiu in the Romanian form: for this was territory disputed over centuries. Edwards held strong views on the Magyar dominance . . .

> *June 28th*—"The native population are mainly of that folk said to have descended from the great days of the Roman Empire, when Transylvania and Walachia formed the province of Dacia; and from whence springs the Romanian language, a Latin dialect. Transylvania withstood the Goth incursions of the Third Century, losing independence only in the Tenth, when the barbarous Magyars swept in from Asia, commencing a struggle for control that— alas for our progressive age—now runs very much

in their favour, though they be a majority merely in a few towns. The Magyars are seen as interlopers, and rightly so; for Transylvania was independent from 1526 to 1699; and many mourn the passing of those wondrous days—be they somewhat tinged with romance—when a noble people held steadfast against Ottoman, Magyar, Saxon and Hapsburg. Transylvania's fate since annexation by the Empire has not been good—except for the Magyars, who through chicanery and bribery have so taken advantage of circumstance and the effete Austrians that they have secured the province's incorporation into Hungary! The Romanians pray the days will not be long for the Empire, and they may not be disappointed. Already, Bismarck is rapping on the doors of Vienna. Indeed, if Austria ever were to fall before a new Prussian Germany—by no means impossible—the game would indeed be up for the arrogant Magyars. There is a legend that a grand Romanian Prince from Transylvania's past will return in the next Millennium to liberate the land; who will reunite the provinces of Transylvania and Walachia, and forge the nation once again into a Great Power."

Julia flipped through the pages of the manuscript. It could date from no earlier than 1867, the year of the *Ausgleich*, when the Magyars secured from the weakened Empire control over Transylvania; not until the 1870s did Romania regain independence, still without the Transylvanian lands. She wondered whether the journal predated or followed her expedition to the Dolomites. The journal continued . . .

"Indeed, it is a great scandal that here in Sibiu the Romanian populace are exiled to the edges of the town that arrogantly boasts the Magyar name—second class citizens in their own land! We are staying at a tavern run by Germans; for the founders of this quaint town—which they call Hermannstadt, resembling, indeed, nothing so much as a small Nuremberg, with narrow streets and ancient, gabled houses—were Saxons. There is a massive cathedral devoted to the Lutheran faith, which has on the north wall of the choir a magnificent Crucifixion by Johannes von Rosenau; in form and colouring, and in the execution of the figures, it exhibits the distinct styles of both Tuscany and Flanders, offering further testimony to this land's history as meeting place of many cultures. In the Bruckenthal Palace, we hear, there are many paintings by Memling, Hals, Rubens, Titian and Lorenzo Lotto; and a library with rare incunabula and many ancient manuscripts.

"Now even the Saxons—though there are more of them—must sing the Magyar tune. So say our hosts, the family Kretzschmar. They are most hospitable. As Lucy is fluent in German, we have enjoyed much the best conversation on our tour so far; and certainly the best fare—the wine in Szolnok was quite undrinkable! Indeed, I cannot but record that, thus far, we have not felt welcome amidst the Hungarians, who regard women travellers as exceedingly strange; we have felt, at times, the butt of a most vulgar humour and unwarranted pestering, on which it would be indecorous to elaborate.

"I must praise our guides since Beiuş, who are not Magyar; being of yet another race amid this patchwork corner of Europe. They are gypsies—confusingly named Roma, yet distinct from the true Romanian. They led us through the wild Bihar passes—alas, in heavy rains that all but hid the summits, apart from one brief, splendid glimpse of Gălina, emerging from swirling, golden mists like a Heavenly vision in a painted ceiling by Correggio. We rode on horses that climbed easily up the gradients with the confident agility of padding cats. We have secured, through the good offices of our hosts, another gypsy team to escort us into the Lotrului Mountains, that south-west of here form part of the vast Carpathian range; then over the high Pasul Vâlcanului, the Vulcan Pass, towards the Walachian flanks; taking then an eastern alpine route, turning northwards up the Gorge of the Oltul to the Pasul Turnu Roşu, the Pass of the Red Tower, and so eventually circling back to Sibiu."

The next entry was made on the far side of the Pasul Vâlcanului in the aftermath of a dreadful storm . . .

July 15th—"Yesterday we crossed the Pasul Vâlcanului, Vulcan's Pass. We had over the previous days made our way through the land that lies between the immense peaks of Cindrel and Ştefleşti. Our weather had been fine, though exceedingly hot, even at night; and we were lucky that our course ran alongside a fully flowing stream. Bears are said to inhabit the region, though we saw none; but we had impressive sights of eagles, coasting on the heat waves, once a pair below us in a deep gorge, such that we looked down on their vast, unfurled wings, glowing in the sunrise.

We are mounted on tough hill ponies, of sure foot, burdened with camping gear and materials for sketching, writing and simple archaeology—though no longer entirely so, for yesterday we were visited by catastrophe and lost much equipment. Indeed, we are lucky to be alive.

"Overnight, temperatures had fallen like a stone, with an immensity and suddenness that astonished, leaving a bitter frost on our tents, and discomforting even our sturdy ponies; yet by noon the dreadful heat of the previous day had returned, this time more sultry. The Pass has an evil reputation amongst the peasants, and had we not already gone so far, rendering return more hazardous than continuing, I am sure even our bold guides would not have risked matters. A tempest of unspeakable ferocity overtook us. It has left one of our guides, a fourteen-year-old boy, injured; while Lucy was almost swept to her death in torrents bursting from a sudden flooding of the Jiul.

"Even at dawn there was an indefinable doom in the air. I half awoke some time before first light; the stars were scintillating in the heavens in multiple images, which I believe to be caused by the icy air. Westward, I could see grim Peleaga, a dark bulk in the starlight, crowned with glinting snow; and his worthy satellites, more craggy and narrow, likewise adorned. There were wolves howling: how near it was hard to estimate, for sounds were sharp in the icy clarity. The boy, Radu, heard too, for he emerged, anxiously it seemed, from his tent; then, seeing me, uttered some words and gesticulated. I saw him cross himself, and turn to face the East. Here they pay allegiance to the Orthodox Church, and are greatly superstitious—though no more than I have known in Italian villages, where the merest icons are worshipped as in a Pagan land.

"I watched in awe as the rising sun—still invisible, for we had camped in an eastern side-valley—tainted the Peleaga group in lurid crimson fire, as if blood seeped from the cracks and crannies. The rose-tinted, snow-dusted peak, and the surrounding aiguilles and precipices, were etched against a bank of churning black cumulus, that would later bring the dreadful storm. The spectacle of the ever-changing light—which in the penumbra looked so many shades of violet—as crimson turned to scarlet, vermillion, magenta and shades of red for which there can surely be no sufficient name, carried with it a hint of the demonic, and yet, simultaneously, paradisiacal. Though the air was icy, already I could sense, like an advancing wall, the awful tempest that was approaching. The prospect disturbed our chaperones, for they went into urgent conference. Eventually, our leader, Dan, came to me, and bade me raise the others. "Rău, rău. Bad, bad," he said, but motioned to go on; it was clear he wished to retreat from the invading murk, rather than linger in its maw. I for one was glad to proceed, as it goes against all in my nature to go back or give up.

"We crossed the Pass soon after one in the afternoon; already, overhead, it was growing as dark as the hour preceding dusk. As we looked back, dismayed, clouds were seething over the cold, a grey, flowing cataract. The air rapidly assumed a torrid weightiness that sapped the very limbs, and made even breathing a trial. A helm of steely-grey hid Peleaga's brow, as if readying for conflict; yet across his southern slopes fell beams of an angry sun, escaping through a rent in the dismal heavens, colouring the mountain's sheer, black precipices in a dread, coppery lustre. Clusters of lesser summits nearby partook of this exhibition, streaks and splashes of the same fiery pigments colouring the wasteland, as if some great slaughter had been done there, in the old days of the world. At last, after insupportable tension, Vulcan's fire seared the firmament, again and again, like sparks shooting from a multitude of Satan's forges; ushering in a downpour such that we could see not a thing before us, and with blasts so terrifying that our ponies were grievously affrighted."

Julia paused, seized by a flicker of *déjà vu*. Had she read something like this before? There were, she supposed, similar passages in her other books. Edwards was mistress of the macabre, poetic image; not for nothing was she renowned as a writer of weird tales and mystery, as well as travelogues. The Victorian imagination tended easily towards melodrama. Such wilderlands were then remote and awe-inspiring in a manner inconceivable today. Edwards's metaphor of ancient slaughter was prescient— it had been surpassed within these very frontiers a hundredfold over the ensuing century.

The next entry was a fortnight later, by which time they had reached the threshold of the Red Tower Pass. There was a mood of doom-laden drama, of terrors insidiously lurking. There was an account of an incident one bright moonlit night that could have been taken from the pages of a Gothic novel . . .

August 2nd—"Tomorrow, with luck, we traverse the Pasul Turnu Roşu—as we regard it now, in the fading sun, how fitting is that name! Since escaping storm and torrent, our journey has continued most ill-favoured. Radu, our boy guide, who was injured in a rock fall that accompanied the tempest, is in great pain—I fear he has a fracture—and has, perforce, to be borne permanently on one of the ponies; we have thus been forced to abandon many supplies, including our remaining sketching materials. My own pony, too, has become lame in one hoof; and I have had to walk long distances over rough terrain, bringing painful blisters. There were several nights, clear and cold, with a near full moon, when we heard wolves again. I must describe one of these, as it was truly disquieting. The legacy, I fear, is with us still.

"We pitched all day up an endless incline, resembling nothing so much as an infinitely sloping stony beach, a shortcut which our guides say will save much time; for they are concerned for the boy, who is their nephew, and wish to get him back to a surgeon in Sibiu. We have almost used up the laudanum we packed for emergencies. Night fell with startling quickness; we must not forget that already it is August and the evenings draw in early.

"The howling began almost as soon as darkness arrived; and, at first, we lacked even the illumination of the moon, which did not arise until midnight. I have to say, the howls gave even me a chill. Sibyl was quite distrait, such that Lucy had to spend an inordinate time consoling her before she slept; and indeed administering, to my displeasure, some precious drops of our depleted laudanum. The guides took extraordinary precautions to prevent the ponies from bolting, creating a kind of pen by driving the beasts into a thicket of severely sharp gorse—which here swathes the hillsides in glorious effusions of golden-yellow, brighter than we see in England.

"At around two o'clock in the morning there was a terrible commotion, as if some wild creature were in torment, so dreadful the noise. I was outside my tent even before our guides, who were supposedly keeping watch. As I stepped into the moonlight I could hear a pitiful crying; and my thoughts immediately went to the boy, whose leg, now swollen badly, is causing him ever more agony. Several hundred yards away, towards the black precipice, I saw a figure, robed in white; it was quite some moments before I realised it was Sibyl, stumbling back towards the tent as if in an hypnotic or somnambulistic state in her nightgown. Lucy was soon at her side, and we heard the story. Sibyl told of a terrible nightmare, of a snuffling outside her tent; and a sense that, though she knew she should lie low, she was impelled, nevertheless, to open the flap. This she did. But, of what occurred next, except that it was terrible, she could not recall. Then, as she came to with that wonderful feeling of relief, when one wakes and knows it was all a dream, what was her terror to find she was lying beneath the precipice, her face and neck all bloody!

"This was, I am certain, a case of sleepwalking (though she claims never to have suffered that affliction before); her bloodied abrasions the result of falling on the stony ground. I have to say I was unhappy at bringing Sibyl on the expedition in the first place, and advised Lucy against. The child is only nineteen and not of a robust constitution; indeed, I would aver, somewhat of an hysterical disposition, prone to childish fancies. She is not at all like the hardy girls Lucy is accustomed to hiring as maids; and whilst, perhaps, suitable for keeping house in London, is unfitted for the wilds. I am not sure, either, that Lucy's affection for her is quite correct in the relations between mistress and servant; indeed, sometimes it is as if Sibyl were mistress, and Lucy maid. It is having a weakening effect on our expedition, though I dread to say so to Lucy.

"Indeed, Sibyl's state is, day by day, becoming a cause for concern; we now travel with two invalids, and Lucy in the role of nursemaid. This afternoon we had to make the crossing of a stream in high spate. At a point where a cataract of astonishing grandeur plunged to level rapids, the guides arranged a handrail of rope, so that we could step across; the spate being too strong to risk riding on the ponies. Lucy herself was, understandably, nervous, but Sibyl was quite impossible, such that even Dan began to lose his equable temper, and virtually dragged her screaming over the water. Once the other side, she collapsed to the ground in a species of fit, as if her swift, short breaths would stop and she would expire, gasping and heaving this way and that, in a manner most distressing; and heedless even of Lucy's entreaties. And more laudanum! I even wonder if she is becoming addicted, for I have heard this can happen with injudicious usage; but Lucy assures me that she alone has been guarding the phial.

"My pony is still lame, but we have had to put Sibyl on his back, for she can barely walk a yard, and seems suffering from a sickness, whether physical or mental I cannot say. I am doubtful whether she can proceed beyond Sibiu, but when I broached this with Lucy, she was quite short with me. As we struggled up the pass, and I looked back upon our ragged company, it was like a scene from ancient legend. Sibyl, mounted on her pony, in white garments, her long, raven hair loose round her shoulders, her blue eyes bright, her lips parted in a distant smile, appeared to me like the Queen of Faerie; and we, the acolytes who serve her, chaperoning her to a great glory. She is, in truth, uncommonly attractive, and was an unwelcome object of Radu's interest until pain distracted him. Our guides, though still the soul of *politesse*, have assumed a certain diffidence. I would like to know what they are discussing, for their tones are grave."

The next substantial entry was not until they had reached Zărneşti, in the Carpathian foothills. A series of short intervening notes showed they had reached Sibiu, staying with the Kretzschmars again until their strength returned. The next leg of their journey was the passage further east into the hinterland of the Făgăraş peaks, and thence over the mountains as far as Bucharest. They made overnight stops in Făgăraş and Braşov, again travelling by stagecoach. In Făgăraş they met an unpleasant reception, attributed by Edwards to their status as female travellers. Stones were thrown, and the police, obliged to rescue them, advised disguise. Their last stop was Braşov, where the Biserica Neagră's "mighty steeples rise to the skies like a multitude of daggers, as if to imitate the jagged peaks and ridges that command the skyline, like portals to the realm of Hades."

August 25th—"Here at Zărneşti Moldoveanu commands the village, and beyond, partly obscured, looms dour Negoiu. Eastward, across a wide gorge, soar the Bucegi peaks, severe in the mornings, yet in the evening, glorious, illuminated in a golden-scarlet glow. Moldoveanu and Negoiu are tipped in snow and must be over 8,000 feet. We, ourselves, are now at several thousand.

"I dread that the return to the wilderland will once again bring on Sybil's fits. Though I remonstrated with Lucy as to the wisdom of continuing with her, she would not entertain leaving her in Sibiu, where, certainly, she appeared to improve somewhat. I myself believe, that, in truth, Sybil is more comfortable as a town-dweller; that she has perhaps been suffering from some form of wilderness anxiety, which can be most potent for certain temperaments. This all goes to vindicate my principal point: she should not have come upon this expedition, and Lucy was much remiss to bring her.

"Yesterday we attended a religious festival for the Virgin—there is much superstition and much blending, as in Italy, of the Christian and the Pagan, in which the Holy Mother of God holds pre-eminence. Great reverence is held for the hawthorn-tree, which grows on the mountain slopes in abundance; the blossom must surely offer gay spectacle in Spring, though even now, with its profusion of carmine berries, it is a sight to behold. The Virgin's shrine was adorned with its fruit, as well as garlic and roses. An infusion brewed from the haw-flowers, supped by worshippers in May, is said to ward off the Devil.

"M. Neguleşcu, our innkeeper—who speaks passable English—told us of an evil spirit prominent in local lore, against whom the hawthorn is deemed efficacious. He named this demon *Vukodlak*— inhabiting the bodies of suicides and other sinners not blessed with Our Lord's Salvation; and who feast nightly on the blood of the innocent, who then become themselves accursed. He told of a dread place further into the hills, beneath sombre crags, a deserted village, where an entire population, within living memory, had been so stricken that it had been necessary to destroy each individual. This is done by driving a stake, fashioned from a hawthorn bole, or stout limb, through the heart, while the evil one rests during the day. There were cousins, even sisters and brothers, he said, who had to perish. My expression of a wish to see the place—for he spoke also of frescos in an ancient chapel—was met, however, with alarm; and it was evident that M. Neguleşcu had not so much been reciting a fascinating piece of lore, as articulating an historical incident of great seriousness. We would not find anyone to take us, he said; and in any case, it would mean negotiating a mountain path long made unsafe by avalanches. I fear he underestimates the resilience of the fairer sex! The superstition of these people is beguiling; they are like children, afraid of the dark—and yet, in their naïve sincerity, as so often with children, their terror is infectious. I was glad Sibyl did not hear the tale."

The women were guided on the next stage of their journey by M. Neguleşcu's nephew, a youth in his twenties, Gabriel. Their immediate destination was the tiny village of Vâla, some thirty miles away, on the plateau separating the domains of Moldoveanu and Negoiu . . .

> *September 2nd*—"Beyond Zărneşti the road climbs through spruce forest; then, narrowing to the merest track, steeply ascends for many miles a rough stony terrain, where only stunted shrubs cling on: hawthorn, rowan, holly, juniper. The region is uncharted, and though we have with us our Mayr and Artaria maps, there are numerous inaccuracies and a lack of correspondence between the two. Everywhere we see shrines, in many cases most elaborate—almost small chapels. Some have stained glass images, in the Orthodox style, and are many hundreds of years old. They are dedicated to St. Anastasia, who is the local protector, with a specific charm against plague and wild beasts. The effort, I am afraid, is again starting to weary Sibyl."

The journal was continued the very next day, towards evening. They were camped on the upland plateau, some dozen miles from Vâla . . .

> *September 3rd*—"Today we have passed through alpine meadows, exquisitely blooming with white campanula, blazing red poppies, violets, edelweiss, ladies' gloves, grape-fern and numerous others, all crowded with such striking density that their weaving colour patterns resemble the most exotic carpets of Persia. The air is like nectar. I feel a great vigour, as if I could scale the summit of Moldoveanu himself.
>
> "Alas, I cannot say the same for either Lucy or Sibyl. In Lucy's case it is anxiety for Sibyl, and

though it brings no practical benefit, I cannot but take satisfaction in my unheeded warnings. Sybil continues to ail, she is very wan, and appears almost the victim of a consumption. Though her eyes glitter, it is not a healthy sign, and she looks sick and starving, scarcely partaking of our modest yet wholesome fare. She is much given to prolonged moods of withdrawal, in which she seems to stare beyond the frontiers of this world. This child is plainly not suitable for the wilds; if her weakness persists, we may be forced to change our plans. I hope it will not come to that, as we are amidst scenery of rare magnificence—albeit of a not quite comfortable kind for some.

"Gabriel insists we make an early start in the morning. Although not far, he wishes to allow a generous margin to ensure arrival by evening, as night gathers fast in the shadow of the mountains. I think he, too, is concerned at the burden Sybil has become; I have noticed him frequently glancing at her with a grave expression in his eyes; or perhaps it is simply youthful ardour, for even as she grows paler, our ailing maid acquires an ever more fragile beauty."

The next date, late September, showed they had lingered longer in Vâla than originally intended. Edwards had made good use of the time, to judge from her detailed notes describing treasures in the church, and her visit to the Convent of the Sisters of the Blessed Sacrament, on a promontory above the village, where she found notable frescos of the Annunciation. The entry appeared to date soon after they had left . . .

September 20th—"We have, at last, departed Vâla, and I rejoice that Lucy has consented to travel on with me, albeit with great reluctance and much cajoling on my part; agreeing only on condition that we return here, instead of proceeding on direct to Bucharest. We have been obliged to leave Sybil behind in the care of the villagers. We had hoped that rest and good food would have restored her to health, but she is much worse. She is in high fever, though her hands and forehead are like ice; and has fallen into a species of delirium, now gloomy, now sad, now joyously hysterical; and at times—this is worst—in mortal trepidation, when she kicks her legs and pushes with her hands, as if to fend off something which she sees that we do not. The innkeeper's wife, Helena, had secured agreement of the Blessed Sisters to hospitalise her in the convent, for the nuns have some medical expertise; but such were her screaming protestations when born to the gates that we had to relent, and have left her in the care of our kind hosts.

"My worry is lest, once we depart, she turn against them; for, on our arrival at the inn, she behaved most irrationally; exhibiting a reluctance, strangely, even to cross its threshold, until M. Cloşca, our landlord, implored her, with kind entreaty, to enter his estimable tavern. They hint at herbal remedies, and seem as concerned as we that she should not walk abroad in her present condition.

"The scent upon the air, as we departed in the dawn, was like the odour of sanctity itself; in this place where, at every corner, some item—a shrine, a window, a statue, an icon, a fresco—reminds us that here we reside under the protection of St. Anastasia.

Anastasia, we are told, was martyred at Sremska Mitrovica in the Balkans in the Fourth Century, and is commemorated by the Roman Catholic Church; which, in this region of Transylvania blends with the Orthodox in the Uniate Church, or Catholic Church of the Eastern Rite, centred in Blaj; and which has been a focus since the Eighteenth Century of Romanian cultural revival, causing, in many parts, frequent persecution. Anastasia is said to have led a life of great danger and adventure, which is why she has been adopted as protector of those in peril of the wild, which here, I must confess, weighs heavy.

"For our journey beyond Zărneşti we were all given by M. Cloşca a medallion of St. Anastasia (much like our St. Christopher, an amulet for safe travel), but Sybil, perverse as ever, discarded hers, claiming its cheap gilt blackened her flesh in a single night. Really! One might think our maid quite the little lady, used to gold and diamonds! We have also been given by the priest at Vâla, M. Mănescu, tiny gold crucifixes, which we understand to be charms of still greater potency than the medallions; which he implored us never to be without. I am afraid I had to tell him a white lie about the cross he gave us for Sybil; for, after the fuss about the medallion, we could not contemplate plying it upon her in her present hysteria. His gift is generous indeed—these crosses are of an antique gold, of which I have never seen the like outside a museum.

"Indeed, never have I seen a place so overwhelmed by crucifixes! During our climb up the steep way to Vâla, we passed more than I have seen even in the most Catholic regions of Bavaria, where this practice is common. The crucifixes here resemble them in their wooden-gabled structure, though the images of the Redeemer are of the Orthodox form, some of exquisite craft. We even heard a legend in the village concerning a silver crucifix kept in the church, said to have been found in the year 1453 in a field hard by, where it was turned up accidentally by a plough. It is thought to have been buried for security; some say during the Barbarian invasions in the Fifth Century, but more likely at the time of the Turkish incursions of the Fifteenth. Since discovery it is supposed to have wrought many miracles, sweated blood and stayed pestilence; and to have protected the village from the depredations of a brutal *voevod*, named Vlad, said to have slaughtered thirty thousand of his own people, and mutilated many more, through vile tortures too hideous to describe here.

"We heard more about Vlad from an old woman, Elisabetha, who has a reputation as a seer. She is credited with the power of prophesy and other magical talents. We were taken to her on our last day by M. Cloşca. It would have been ill-mannered to refuse. Elisabetha is in her nineties and is blind, having been so since birth; but possessing that uncanny ability to sense a presence, and even move around complicated arrangements of objects as if actually perceiving them. Over endless cups of a strong herbal tea she regaled us with many tales of superstition.

"Here in Vâla, the wicked Vlad exceeds all other bogeymen, rivalling even Turk and Magyar. That Vlad was truly a native prince, as some allege, was, Elisabetha says, untrue: his sires invaded millennia

144

before, coming from the Russian steppes, in the form of rabid white wolves, preserved in the local fable of the 'Murony'—men who change by night into ferocious hounds. Though Vlad battled valiantly against Turk and Saxon, too many today speak recklessly of invoking this old devil, so as to break, once and for all, the yoke of Buda-Pesth. Elisabetha told of a recurring dream, visiting her since her teens, in the guise of a prophesy: that in the next millennium Antichrist himself will arise in the West, beyond Bohemia and Moravia, and lay waste the Eastern lands; that traitors will arise and sell the people's soul; that, though Antichrist be stalled on his battlefield, his devastation will live on for many a generation; and amongst the dreadful consequences will be the frenzied ravages of the Russian Bear; and that one, a son of Satan, shall arise, and take the throne of Transylvania and Walachia, posing as a hero of his people, who with his evil wife will amass great gold, yet bleed the nation dry, inflicting untold death and suffering, torture and starvation, and deadly plague—the very reincarnation of Vlad, whose foul progeny are said to lie, always sleeping, yet sleepless, in ruined fortresses and mausoleums throughout the land.

"Elisabetha seemed to know already of Sybil's indisposition (though hardly second sight in so small a community). On no account, she warned, should we abandon Sibyl, for her soul was in peril. Her final words, accompanied by the sign of the cross and a curious jabbing with two fingers, were to counsel prudence on our journey; and a vigilance, especially, with regard to the wolves that run beneath Negoiu.

"We have, much to our chagrin, lost Gabriel as our guide; for he was cheerful company and spoke good English. He had promised to stay with us, but affected a sudden change of mind. We never learned his reason; he offered too many excuses to sound convincing, though we parted on cordial terms."

The diary's next entry was in October . . .

October 9th—"Not far beyond Vâla we came upon one of the small wooden churches that are a feature of the country; the door, unfortunately, was locked. We could see through a window two strange frescos, which the early sun illuminated. I would say, from their demeanour, that they depict saints; yet one has the head of a wolf, the other, which is female, the head of an owl. My guess is that the owl represents Anastasia, for among her many properties is said to be wisdom; the other is probably St. Christopher, a saint of universal importance throughout the Balkans, sharing many of Anastasia's roles—though it is puzzling that a saint who keeps the wild things at bay should himself be shown in the guise of a carnivorous beast; for it conjured little sense of Christian Salvation. What Sybil would have done had she seen it, I tremble to imagine!

"I, for one, have tried to banish Sibyl from my mind; for all such sentiment is unproductive, and we must make the best of our time if we are to complete our trip before Winter.

"We did not find it easy to procure another guide. In the end, Filip agreed to lead us. He is half Roma, and has been a shepherd all his life, knowing every stone of these hills; he is in his seventies, but hardly looks a day past fifty. He is a silent character—he has few words in English. Lucy is unduly quiet too: daily she thinks of Sibyl, being afflicted by a great remorse, most futile of emotions!

"I noticed Lucy no longer had on the exquisite ruby ring she always wears. It belonged to her mother, and is antique. When I enquired, she admitted, with some discomfiture, that she had given it as a parting gift to Sybil. I trust that this, at least, will not turn her flesh black! For it is set in platinum, and priceless. I was very sharp with Lucy, and reminded her that Sibyl was only a maid. A tension grows between us, I fear.

"Filip has a shotgun, and I must profess that we are glad—for many a night we have heard wolves howling, mercifully distant. We have dined well on rabbit, hare, pheasant and other fowl, which Filip downs with a marksman's eye. There are many chamois, delightful, agile creatures, bounding over the roughest terrain with the ease of a bird in the air. These our hunter will not kill, for they are deemed sacred. A more desolate place, however, cannot be imagined than the black corries beneath Negoiu, which suck the light of day, rather than gain illumination from it. Not even chamois stray there, says our shepherd-guide; nor did we, ourselves, linger long.

"Like all peasants, he is superstitious; this was revealed most forcibly when we encountered, on the edge of a pine forest underneath foreboding cliffs, a small church in decayed condition. It stood in a glade of young hawthorn. I wanted to know whether this was the site of the stricken village M. Neguleşcu said had to be purged. I would say from Filip's objections when I evinced a wish to investigate, that this is so. Nevertheless, I proceeded, and what reward! Here, indeed, were frescos of great age, and of high order, albeit ravaged by age and weather. I have little time to give the full description they merit—for we must soon make grave decisions concerning our future route; but I must set down some thoughts while the awesome impact is fresh in my mind.

"There is a trio of panels with life-size figures. One, the best preserved, shows a gruesome martyrdom—a female saint, Anastasia, possibly? The detail, for all that it serves some pious allegory, is unspeakably hideous. The second—the Madonna and Child—is grievously damaged, damp and dereliction having done their worst. Though the quality of the drawing rivals Giotto, the colour has faded from the flowing garments; worst of all, the face of the baby Jesus is so defiled as to leave the impression of an unholy leer, imparting to the whole an aspect of the profane rather than the sacred. The third panel—an angel battling a demon—has much missing; most especially, the top left-hand corner, where once the fiend's face would have shown, yet the wings and talons are sufficient to terrify, suggesting a blasphemous creature of night. Most distressing is the look upon the angel's face, of valour thwarted, sureness of defeat, in which the whole Christian message seems to falter. I left the church in a mood that comprised both wonder and revulsion. It is as if, in this forsaken land, the Christian flock dwell not so much on the Lamb of God, as on the challenge of the Evil One."

There was one more entry, the narrative cutting out on a climactic note . . .

October 15th—"We have been here now, in the very heart of this wilderness, for three days, paralysed not by weather or other natural discomfort, but by debate about our future path; and I fear that, if I wish to carry on, it will be alone. Lucy and Filip, for different reasons, are resolved to go no further. Lucy, in truth, has not been herself at all since leaving Vâla—all because of that foolish maid! She continues plagued by guilt, last night breaking down in tears—which was most unaccustomed. She has been having frightful dreams that dissipate on waking, concerning matters affecting Sibyl, a form of premonition, that she is in mortal peril; and, indeed, may even have passed beyond the confines of this world. It is most grievous that so sensible a companion, assuming in the past an hauteur towards such things, should have fallen into craven superstition. It is as if she, too, has been seduced by the fancies of our guide, who beneath his rugged veneer exhibits, in this respect, great timidity. He was not pleased at my defiance over visiting the church; I fear I have broken some taboo, and am now branded as a bearer of calamity. I am sure it is only his estimable sense of honour that has kept him with us these past few days, while Lucy and I argue endlessly.

"I am seated, as I write these words, it seems, on the very edge of the world. We have reached an upland plateau, where the highest peaks still tower, yet sufficiently proximate to enclose, oft times creating the sensation, especially as night falls, that we are trapped in a labyrinth of gloom. Our way back is clear enough, at least to Filip—should we so decide. Ahead is more uncertain. But that is of the essence, surely? To break new ground and make discovery! I am gazing over a vast precipice, beyond which the land plunges vertiginously. Pine and spruce forest spreads below, a blackish-green canopy, which, nevertheless, glimmers in the early morning sun. Mountains innumerable stretch to the horizon, yet even the highest bears no name upon our maps. In the middle distance looms one that has brought us to contention.

"It is a very singular mountain—one of the most singular and the most striking that we have seen on our tour. It is like the front of a vast Gothic cathedral, with one slender aiguille, like a flagstaff, shooting up from the top of one of its crenellated towers; and, surrounding, many savage crags and precipices, arêtes and pinnacles, the very battlements of Hell! In form it is most unlike its neighbours, amidst which it rises in defiant isolation. It is very difficult to judge its distance, and, therefore, true height; but it is near enough to glimpse, on a lower cliff, massive ruins, one of the great Saxon fortresses from the days of the Turkish invasions.

"Lucy saw the mountain first, as we emerged from forest, dominating in a manner most arresting and conspicuous. It has filled her with a dread from which no retreat has proven possible. Perhaps it speaks of a vaster wildness, a greater strangeness beyond; for the fear of wilderland has now infected her, I fear. She is determined to return to Vâla, and to Sybil. Filip, too, behaved curiously. When I asked him (though I am never sure he fully understands) the name of this outlandish peak, he affected ignorance as to which I meant; and this despite its commanding the entirety of the immediate view. Pressed, he would not yield, muttering words to the effect that 'over that way lay Walachia, he did not go there'. I suppose we have reached the limit of his terrain. I fear we have come to the parting of our ways. I, myself, have only felt my enthralment whetted—as much by the mystery in which this unknown mountain is enveloped, as by its grim contours.

"Filip advises—and I feel sure this is but a pretext—that the land falls too steeply to carry on; but there is a way I see to the right: a lengthy descent down a rocky shoulder that would lead us to the ravines and forests below. After that, even with the most generous estimates of distance, it cannot be more than . . . "

Here the manuscript ceased.

Julia flicked pointlessly at the final page; the anticlimax was numbing. She had become caught up in the narrative, so authentically evocative. She put the journal down and made more coffee.

Something at the back of her mind bothered her, something to do with the account of the strange mountain. It was oddly familiar, as if she had read something like it before. She reached for *Untrodden Peaks* and thumbed through.

On page eighty-nine she located a sketch: "Unknown mountains near Cortina". On the next page she read: "Now it was a very singular mountain—one of the most singular and the most striking that we saw throughout the tour." Almost identical! The account went on to record the response of the locals when pressed to name it; their reaction was similar to Filip's, vague disclaimers that they had "not noticed it before", that they did not go there, it was "*della parte d'Italia*". Julia searched further: on page 125 was the vivid metaphor of ancient slaughter, inspired by Cristallino and the Croda Rossa in the Dolomites, in the diary by the Peleaga massif—a single phrase, but clearly lifted. There were other minor replications, such as the likening of an alpine meadow to a Persian carpet. And here, on page 132, was a close version of the tale of the miracle-working crucifix!

Julia felt suddenly uneasy. Was the diary a fake? The work of a plagiarist? Imagine if she had advertised it as genuine—it didn't bear thinking about. She double-checked the handwriting. There could be no mistake. Had the author, then, plagiarised her own work? But why do that? One would hardly transcribe one's own publication into a spontaneously written diary? Was it, then, the other way round? Had scenes witnessed on an unrecorded Carpathian expedition later been incorporated, with immense poetic license, into *Untrodden Peaks and Unfrequented Valleys*? Julia's mind swirled in confusion.

She wondered what to do with the manuscript. Unless a credible solution to the puzzle were found, and provenance established, it was a bit of a pig in a poke. She must be careful not to make a fool of herself. The antiquarian book trade was merciless.

Over the ensuing weeks the riddle never left her mind. She sought out other writings by Edwards, including a reprint of her supernatural tales by a small publishing house in Canada. She found the stories somewhat predictable, but Julia was impressed by the author's vivid evocation of landscape—as compelling as her travelogues. Edwards had a sure command of *genius loci*, imbuing her stories with a verisimilitude that stemmed from mastery of scenic description, as well as an eye for the eerie: the Black Forest; a Venetian graveyard; a lonely church on the Upper Rhine; the Swiss Alps—all plausibly transformed into stages for supernatural dramas . . .

With a creeping conviction, Julia began to suspect what the manuscript was. She was not sure whether she was pleased . . .

Here, surely, was the handwritten draft of an unpublished supernatural tale? A vampire story—a quarter-century before Bram Stoker. Edwards had transcribed real incidents from her Dolomite tour, including the magnificent metaphor of bloody slaughter, the crucifix legend and the vista of a sinister mountain fortress, into the medium of a Gothic tale. It was disappointing to relinquish the prospect of having discovered a record of an unknown expedition. On the other hand, a Carpathian vampire tale predating Stoker was of considerable import. It might well prove lucrative; the prices fetched by supernatural rarities were even more preposterous than those achieved by travel books. It was a pity it was not complete. Possibly, Edwards had written more, been dissatisfied and torn out the later pages. Even incomplete, it would have a price.

※

It was mid-June when Julia arrived in Sibiu, following a short flight from Bucharest over the mist-shrouded Carpathians.

Edwards, she had decided, must actually have visited the region to have written the account in the first place. That was how she worked: transforming reality, places she had visited, through the alchemy of prose into fiction. The diary exhibited a knowledge that seemed only possible from first hand experience, neither derivative nor invented. From the moment Julia entered the old town at Sibiu, it was as if she stepped into the pages of the manuscript.

Sibiu, despite the drab apartment blocks, had still a medieval charm. In the huge Evangelical Cathedral she found the Rosenau crucifixion that had so impressed Edwards. A train took her through Făgăraş, scene of the women's humiliation. *The Rough Guide to Romania* did not have much time for the place either: "scarred by chemical works and communist attempts at town planning". Reaching Zărneşti, Julia became ever more convinced she was journeying in Edwards's footsteps. The local tourist office, however, could shed no light on the village of Vâla; nor was it marked on any map. The best she could find was a clue in a leaflet on local lore: a deserted village beneath a ruined convent where the population had been devoured by wolves more than a century ago.

Beyond Zărneşti she passed many shrines and crucifixes, even as Edwards had described. The area grew thick with hawthorn, decked in dazzling white midsummer bloom. High on a rocky spur were grey ruins—was this the convent, the site of Vâla? The scenery was exquisite, with graceful birch, oak, beech, spruce and pine; and many alpine blooms, including acres of wild white garlic, its rank scent heavy on the sweet mountain air. The land continued rising, over rough ground, past tumbling cataracts and isolated stands of trees. At last, in a late June twilight, she beheld the awesome, soaring black crags of Negoiu.

Truly Edwards had captured the grand, uncanny scene. Foreboding peaks loomed above dark cliffs and corries; where birds of prey and chamois were her sole companions over leagues of shattered rock; where twilight conjured up a world in which all manner of demons could be imagined to lurk. Counsels of caution had been offered in Zărneşti: about bears, wild boars and wolves, about uncharted wildernesses, about perilous crumbling edifices hidden away in the hills. As she stepped further and further into the scene of the narrative, the borderline between fact and fiction continued to dissolve. One old man, when she asked directions, had even made the sign of the cross.

Julia pitched tent. As a safety precaution she suspended her food supplies in a pine tree; if bear or wolf came scavenging, they would be lured away from the tent.

The peaks were already bathed in the rose-pink light of dawn when Julia arose. The air was pleasantly cool, its scent like the bouquet of a precious wine. By ten o'clock she had made good distance, veering south. Not another soul had she met in two days.

As the afternoon advanced, the land became more wooded. Dark conifers climbed the slopes, up to scree and crag. Endless pinnacles and peaks soared on either side, their forms and shadows shifting in the ever-changing light. Old ruins in a hawthorn glade beside a spruce wood made her wonder whether here it was that Edwards found the church with the ravaged frescos. Several miles of thickening forest, and the land abruptly opened up. Twilight was gathering.

Julia was suddenly transfixed . . .

A strange-looking mountain commanded the horizon— like an immense, shattered Gothic cathedral. *Now it was a very singular mountain—one of the most singular and the most striking that we saw throughout the tour.*

Julia's mind whirled. Her first intuitions had been right: the image of the weird summit in the Dolomites, in *Untrodden Peaks*, was apocryphal—Edwards had seen this dread peak in the Carpathians.

The mountain was not so large as first appeared; higher summits ranged to right and left, such that it stood in grim seclusion. But whatever it lacked in height, it more than made up for in rugged severity: the splintered crags, the arêtes and pinnacles, one single, slender aiguille rising like a flagstaff from its shattered summit; and, on its lower slopes, the ruins of a vast fortress on the edge of an abyss. The height was exaggerated by the angle of the ascending plateau, which terminated in a sudden precipice. From the wood, it had appeared to tower alone against the sky; yet from the edge could be seen still more mountains, extending ever onwards, fading into the distant haze of the evening's glow.

The precipice was like the frontier of an alien realm, the very edge of the world. Julia surveyed the ethereal scene, the dying rays picking out myriad crags and spires. The sun itself was hidden by a high, rocky shoulder that descended steeply to her right, levelling slightly before it dropped to ravines some thousand feet below. This, presumably, was the ridge down which Edwards believed she had espied a route. On the dark side of the dusk, the ridge was a black silhouette.

Julia made camp on the skirts of the forest, craving solace against the wasteland. In the wells of the star-spangled night, the constellations near enough to touch, she felt a terrifying loneliness; she wished she'd left some indication of her intentions in Zărneşti. A pale moon was on the rise. Her food, again, she hung from a tree at a respectable distance. There were stealthy noises she prayed weren't bears or wolves. A spate of howling in the early hours alarmed her; but it was far away, over the precipice.

In the magnificence of the dawn Julia scrutinised the ridge. The top stretch, rough and steeply sloping, looked bad, but the rest appeared no more than a weary trudge. By six she was on her way. She left her tent pitched, intending to return by evening; the long midsummer day was ahead.

The trek took longer than expected. It was already afternoon by the time Julia reached the mountain's boulder-strewn slopes. It was, indeed, formidable. It soared up to the skies, its blackness looming. Huge screes plunged beneath sheer crags that seemed to crumble visibly before her eyes. High above, on a tumbling precipice, perched the ancient Saxon fortress. It was on a scale and in a situation that made its construction unimaginable. A curving track led upwards through pines. It was near her estimated time for safe return; but she had come so far—the imperative of exploration beckoned.

Julia soon realised she had made a big mistake.

The path petered out before insurmountable crags. The weather was changing, the clear blue day turning sultry, copper-tinted clouds massing round the pinnacles, mist swirling in the gullies like a witch's cauldron. Away south were prolonged angry rumbles. Anxiously she essayed a hurried descent, but attempts to navigate directly down through the trees were foiled. The slope became steep, then precipitate, then impassable. She doubled back, with diminishing sense of direction and accelerating panic. Time haemorrhaged away. It was almost dusk before she could hazard a guess as to where she was—way off course. Above, an impenetrable veil of mist swathed the heights.

Ahead, Julia espied crumbling masonry, a kind of old chapel. The architecture was ponderous, probably Saxon like the fort; the stone a dirty yellowish ochre. In the low sun's rays it shone—a sickly, lurid glow—against an iron-grey sky. Thunder boomed, nearer now, prolonged, cacophonous. The air was getting suffocating. Stray drops of rain fell, presaging worse. Unmistakably this time, she heard the baying of a wolf, by no means so far off. She entered the ruin. It was not enticing—but better shelter for the night than dark woods or bare mountainside.

A foul miasma met her. On the floor lay scattered bones. Was this the lair of an animal? The place exuded an air of formidable decay, a grisly commentary on the perishing of all things. The area immediately inside was roofless, but on the far side a rusted metal gate, hanging from one hinge, led into abysmal darkness.

A last stray beam suddenly dispelled the gloom. Beyond the gate was a crypt, a mausoleum. Numerous caskets lay about; or more exactly, lay littered about as if disordered by a natural disaster, a flood or an earth tremor—or else vigorously plundered. One was leaning almost upright, its lid slightly ajar, like an unshut door. There was a rustling and a scuffling behind her.

Julia faced the encroaching figure, haloed by the dying sun. It was a young woman, but a woman so emaciated as to suggest unspeakable disease. She was clad in filthy white draperies that might once have graced a princess: silk, taffeta and muslin, greened with mould. There were brownish stains around the neckline. Her long raven locks were flecked with steely-grey, unwashed, unkempt. Her ruby lips were parting, almost snarling—or in readiness for voluptuous kissing. A soft lapping noise came from her long, rolling tongue. Her eyes glinted eagerly. Julia didn't know whether she was being propositioned or menaced. There was about her a pale, fragile beauty.

Julia recoiled. The folly of her expedition, alone here in the wilderness, besieged her. Was the girl a vagabond, living feral in the wild? Some wastrel of a dislocated society? God forbid! She had read about such things, here in the realms of a failed communist paradise. A junkie, maybe? The waif's glittering blue eyes spoke of addiction, or worse—an immense, merciless hunger. And a graverobber too, by the look of it. The girl was raising her left hand. It flashed in the sun's last glimmer. An exquisite ruby ring dangled loosely from her bony finger. It matched her irresistible red lips.

Nostalgia, Death and Melancholy

*"On every new thing there lies already
the shadow of annihilation."*

– *W. G. Sebald,* The Rings of Saturn

It was nostalgia, perhaps, which brought Sinclair back
to the island; nostalgia and the funeral of his last
immediate relative, his mother's elder sister, Aunt
Lois. It must have been nigh on forty years since he had
last set foot there, with his father and mother. Then the
island had been in its heyday, a haven for working-class
holidaymakers before economy jets and package tours
lured the hoards away to warmer, more exotic climes.
Now it was quiet, faded, melancholy—a tax retreat for the
wealthy and sundry multi-national companies. Nostalgia,
death and melancholy: hardly fine fare for a holiday or for
Sinclair's somewhat morose temperament. And there was
something more: ill-defined, scarcely recognised, a pale
and ominous destiny.

Aunt Lois, ninety-five years old and widowed three
decades, had long outlived her siblings, of whom his
mother, Grace, had been the youngest and the first to
die; Sinclair had only been in his twenties. His father,
having married a woman scarcely older than Sinclair
himself (whom his son heartily disliked), had emigrated
to Australia. Thereafter, their relations had been spare, not

to say estranged until his father's death there of a stroke in the ferocity of the noonday sun ten years later; and Sinclair had edited from his mind the memories of what, he had to admit, had been a contented childhood.

Sinclair was the only heir to Aunt Lois's estate (ignoring a small legacy to the Cats Protection League); though it proved to be something of a white elephant: a five-storey guest house with, as the advertising brochures used to put it, "indirect frontage to the promenade". The days had long gone since Cragmore's crumbling, stuccoed portals regularly bore the sign "no vacancies", but Aunt Lois had apparently been content to preside with Olympian detachment as the once august hotel's ineluctable decline matched her own. Useless either as holiday home or commercial enterprise, his aunt's solicitors had advised accepting a knock-down offer from a firm of local developers, skilled in the conversion of such properties into apartments for the island's abundant *nouveaux riches*; indeed, it would not even be necessary for him to come over. But Sinclair, who normally abhorred even the shortest journey, felt himself under a curious—and not quite comfortable—compulsion.

※

As the sea-cat surged into the broad curve of the bay, Sinclair could not but recall, with pangs of regret, the elegant, romantic ferries of his youth. It was immediately evident, too, that the island—this playground of his early years—had succumbed to an inglorious new age. Many of the impressive hotels along the promenade had been replaced by Costa Brava-style apartment blocks. The picturesque setting of the harbour lighthouse had been ravaged by an ugly new link-span for the ferry. Where the Pavilion Theatre once stood a glass-fronted bank struggled to imitate Art Deco. Never go back, Sinclair reflected. A dullness, bordering on malaise, gripped his soul. *Sic transit gloria mundi*. A fine, persistent rain had begun to fall.

It had been agreed, by arrangement with the solicitors, that Sinclair would sojourn, for the few days he expected to be over, in Cragmore itself. There was no urgency about the sale, they assured him; and there were his aunt's not inconsiderable effects to sort through and dispose of as appropriate. There appeared little of significant value, the slick young man on the phone had explained, mainly tack from the forties and fifties, though there were one or two items of furniture; and the firm (evidently as well-connected with the local antique trade as with the property developers) would be happy for a suitable fee to handle the matter. Additionally, some of the deceased's friends had politely expressed an interest even in the worthless items, no doubt craving some memento, she having been a popular character on the island's whist and bridge circuit; doubtless he would meet them at the funeral and could make his own arrangements. And there were all the usual papers, photographs and personal miscellany he might wish to peruse at his leisure. A next-door neighbour, Mrs. Dragon, held a set of keys.

Sinclair, whose instinctive rule in life was to avoid unnecessary bother, was only too glad to fall in with prearranged plans; though he was shrewd enough to realise that Judson, Platt & Olsen could sniff an easy killing.

The prospect of his return to the island unleashed a plethora of poignant, conscience-stricken memories; and much of the journey had been given over to morbid contemplation. In the arrogant immortality of youth he had never taken seriously his mother's illness until the final days; while the estrangement from his father, he now realised, had much to do with Sinclair's own selfishness. An only child, he had been pampered and celebrated without stint by his parents, as well as by numerous benevolent aunts and uncles, all now with the passing of Aunt Lois the dust of memory. The longer he thought, the more remarkable seemed the happiness of his childhood days; and he wished now he had savoured them more at the time, as if by carefully cherishing them he could somehow have delayed the relentless depletion of the hour-glass. Aunt Lois, though scarcely crediting a passing thought in years, symbolised the last link to his parents and his past, indeed quite possibly to everything. *Nostalgia, Death and Melancholy.*

It was astonishing how much forgotten detail flooded back: places they had visited, trivial incidents, snatches of conversation, laughter, sounds and smells. And fixing slowly in his mind, like the magical emergence of a photographic print, was one elusive image in particular: a small rocky cove with an old wooden chalet, reached by a lengthy walk through a narrow, wooded glen with waterfalls and rustic bridges, a place for some unexplained reason especially favoured by his parents. Always, Sinclair recalled, it was here he was most lovingly indulged and their mood at its brightest; but, though the scene now flashed before him with eidetic clarity, its name and location hovered frustratingly just beyond the brink of recollection. Whatever else he did, Sinclair resolved, he would make an effort to rediscover this sacred grove; it would be a mission, a tribute, a pilgrimage.

X

Cragmore's frontage to the promenade proved even more indirect than Sinclair remembered. A huge block of flats, testifying to a certain laxity in the island's planning regulations, loomed across the narrow street, overshadowing the once popular hotel. Aunt Lois had made her home on the lower ground floor; it looked reasonably comfortable for his purposes. He chose a bedroom at the rear, affording an attractive view of a flower-festooned cliff and a tiny garden fringed with blooming palm trees. Their heady aroma drifted evocatively through the windows, summoning up vague impressions, as annoyingly out of reach as the name of the cove.

A brief tour of the upper floors confirmed that from no room was it now possible to see the bay. The eerie vacancy of the once bustling hotel left Sinclair with a sad, disquieted feeling. There was mildew on the wallpaper. The roof had leaked in an attic and been inexpertly repaired. Everywhere was a burgeoning smell of damp, disuse and decay. Once upon a time, countless "bright young things" from his parents' generation had turned these drab corridors alive with excitement, made careless love in the bedrooms, laughed and caroused through days and nights of an endless summer. Almost, Sinclair thought, if you listened closely, you could hear the distant strains of their laughter, the cries of their love-making. His reverie was broken by the harsh screeching of gulls outside as they swooped to fight over some nameless carrion. The gloom of the upper regions hung, appallingly, like a dead weight over him even after his return to the fussily comfortable surrounds of Aunt Lois's quarters.

Already, within an hour of arriving, several of his aunt's acquaintances (alerted, no doubt, by the next-door guardian of the keys) had descended, amiably introducing themselves, their roving eyes greedily surveying the

Aladdin's Cave. Let the vultures choose their pickings, he thought indifferently, as he engaged in pleasantries and made suitable faces at their eulogies, sincere no doubt, to Aunt Lois's fair play at cards.

Consequently, it was rather late when he pushed away the remains of his meal and drained the dregs of the claret he had found in the kitchen. All his aunt's papers, the solicitors had told him, were in a large Victorian writing desk, situated in an office which in better days had served as reception. On top of the desk—old habits died hard—was this season's tourist-board brochure. Sinclair, thinking he might as well find out what was going on these days, picked it up, together with various papers and photographs, retiring to the lounge with a glass of whisky. The stress of the day's impressions and the uncomfortable sea crossing had left him restless, far from sleep. The funeral was not until one o'clock, so it did not matter if he stayed up late and overslept. At the very least, he could make a start on the papers, secure in the knowledge that all important legal documents were most decisively in the hands of Judson, Platt & Olsen.

First, he leafed through the tourist information, which offered tawdry confirmation of the island's descent from grace. A health and fitness club in the former Crescent Cinema. An internet café in Felice's ice cream parlour. Big screen sport and karaoke—God preserve us!—at the Harbour Hotel. Sundry crass enter-tainment to suit the contemporary short attention span . . . Sinclair was about to push the material aside when something struck a familiar chord . . . It was amazing . . . Could it still be running? . . . After all these years?

Not only was the Emerald Coast Electric Railway still operating, it was celebrating its centenary. Sinclair had forgotten all about the old tramway that clambered in and out of the craggy eastern coastline, surmounting seemingly impossible gradients on its thirty-mile journey to the island's northern point. Curiously antiquated even when he was a boy, it was almost unbelievable that it should have survived an era of plummeting tourism, philistine planning and the depredations of the motor car. According to the brochure, it had reaped the generosity of a belated heritage revival, saved in the nick of time by lottery cash. The *fin de siècle* trams, modelled on prototypes that once scaled the precipitous slopes of San Francisco, were apparently the oldest operating examples in the world. The railway in its time had been a revolutionary new technology, a state-of-the-art transportation system, a wonder of the Edwardian world; it had even pioneered the introduction of electricity on the island. In its halcyon days it had been a major tourist enterprise, with numerous attractions emerging along its lengthy route. Amongst these were the "Glens"—narrow, wooded creeks weaving down to tiny coves, studded with rustic benches, illuminations, cafeterias and side-shows. Several had still been there when Sinclair was a child, descending though they were even then into seediness and shabbiness; pale, unprepossessing memorials to a dwindling era.

Suddenly it came to him: Grindle Glen. That was the name of the place that had so enthralled his parents. How could he have forgotten? It was marked on the brochure's illustrated map of the line. But his excitement was as swiftly tempered: Grindle Glen, it stated, was now in private hands and closed to the public, though access to the shore was still assured along the "Old Smuggler's Path". A disproportionate disappointment possessed him. Nevertheless, it would still be worth taking a ride on the line and trying to find the beach.

Aunt Lois's papers proved unremarkable, but amongst them was a box of old photographs. Sinclair rummaged through them. Most were of people he had never known or did not recognise. Some had inscriptions on the back, mostly cryptic. There were all the usual things: wedding snaps; babes and children; waving, grinning people, obviously on holiday; scenes from the island in the background. His aunt and uncle appeared in absurd, inconceivable youth: alone or together, embracing, fooling around or self-consciously serious. He marvelled at his aunt's sexy looks: slim, elegant and athletic, her dark curled hair tied back with a chic head-scarf like in an old Hollywood movie, always laughing. Here was their wedding, neatly card-framed and tissue-protected, also showing his parents, scarcely more than teenagers. Older photos, brown and worn, depicted earlier family groups, Aunt Lois and his mother looking very alike as little girls. There were many of his mother and father on holiday, even some of himself as a babe-in-arms or a surly youngster.

One picture gave him quite a start.

The lens of memory found still deeper focus. He must have been about seven years old. The picture had been taken in the cove at the foot of Grindle Glen. It had occasioned some mild amusement on his father's part; yet Sinclair had found it anything but amusing. He wondered what had happened to his parents' copy; he had not set eyes upon it since he was a boy. It showed himself drying off on the verandah of the old chalet. There must have been something wrong with the film or the camera, an intrusion of light or a processing defect. For, looming over was a blurred, amorphous shape, a parody of a human form but much too tall, clad in what looked like voluminous garments. There was an animation in the figure that made it appear as if it were about to enfold Sinclair within its robes. He recalled being both fascinated and afraid, and not liking the way his father had laughingly called it the "Grindle Ghost". "G for ghost, G for Grindle," he had chanted; Sinclair could hear his voice now, echoing down the years.

Now, in the fading light of Aunt Lois's parlour, with only the distant, muffled sounds of the street, the floodgates of Sinclair's memory breached open. Recol-lections came back with exhilarating clarity of the countless happy days he and his parents had whiled away in the beauty of the little cove. Often they had the place to themselves. The chalet, nestling in a wilderness of brambles, bindweed and honeysuckle on the edge of the pebbled beach, they had appropriated for their own use; no one knew to whom it belonged, and if it was indeed private, nobody seemed to bother. It was remarkable just how frequently it appeared in the photographs. There were several of his mother holding him as a baby, maternal pride in her smile as if posing before a family home. Another of all three together in which the infant Sinclair was looking anxiously behind his shoulder.

Regarding the photos now, decades later, the details of the scene reformed in Sinclair's mind with all the vividness of childhood. The cabin's musty, overheated smell of sun-drenched wood, fusing with the background scents of summer and the sea, surged evocatively back. The chalet always seemed to be the subject of a private joke between his parents. "We'll tell you about it one day," his father once declared, at which his mother, laughing, had said, "I don't know about that!"

Now, skimming back through the discarded pile of photographs, Sinclair felt himself on the brink of a truth, dimly shaping in his mind. There it was: his mother and father, arms round each other, standing on the verandah, laughter in their eyes. He re-read the inscription on the rear: "To Lois and Jack. With thanks, again, for a *lovely* holiday last summer. We knew you'd be delighted at our news. And in memory of a *very special day*! July 29th, 1952. With love from Grace and Tom." Sinclair did a rough calculation. It was just nine months before he had been born. A shiver passed over him. Now he knew why he was being called back. The focus was complete.

※

The Ancient Chapel of Lynass, where his aunt had worshipped, was on the far side of the bay. Here were the wealthier suburbs. Instead of decaying Edwardian terraces, there were broad, tree-lined avenues, flanked by fine villas dating from the island's inter-war prosperity. Most were set back in glorious mature gardens. Hanging on the air was the sensuous, yet nauseous, scent of palm blossom; so similar to the scent of the lilies on his aunt's coffin. As the cortège neared the church, one building, older than the others, caught Sinclair's attention. It was elegantly styled, with a steeply sloping grey slate roof descending two-thirds of the height to white walls, in which were set mullioned windows, repeated dormer-style at intervals along the roof. The edifice was crowned by a graceful open pinnacle and two tapering white chimney-stacks. An arched entrance porch was visible behind ornamental iron gates opening onto the avenue. It was of modest size and looked as if it might be some kind of a parish hall. It looked turn-of-the-century.

Sinclair's interest sharpened. Could it be so? Here, he was sure, was an example of the work of the architect, John Mace-Hopkins. Mace-Hopkins was undergoing something of a revival, in which his own university was involved. Mace-Hopkins had been an intimate of William Morris and John Ruskin and was now seen as one of the principal forces in the Arts and Crafts Movement. Most of his work was to be found in the North Lancashire area. He was also known to have designed a number of buildings on the island, where he had lived for a time. It was surmised there might be other, forgotten examples extant. Could this, mused Sinclair, be one of the lost gems?

Hopes of a new discovery were quickly dispelled; in fact, at the funeral itself. Aunt Lois's burial in the grounds of the Ancient Chapels was followed by refreshments in the very building he had been admiring. It was indeed the local parish hall; and it was, he soon discovered, designed by Mace-Hopkins. This he learned from another funeral guest: Ronald Dykes, a local historian. Not only was Mace-Hopkins's work well-known, but thanks to his own private researches identification of all the architect's work on the island was virtually complete. Dykes was aware of the research going on at Sinclair's university; he had held back his own findings, as he wanted to write them up first for *The Lynass Enquirer*. Dykes, it transpired, had a set of keys to the hall; and, a mutual sympathy established, they agreed to meet again that evening for a conducted tour and a pint in the local inn.

✗

Dykes was a mine of fascinating information, clearly a man of considerable scholarship, with encyclopaedic knowledge of the island. He talked with accelerating enthusiasm as the evening passed and the ale flowed. He had, however, an annoying fault: a distinct preference for the sound of his own voice, with an irritable reaction if interrupted.

Before adjourning to the pub, they had toured the parish hall. Dykes identified the numerous delights of Mace-Hopkins's style. Especially good was the tile-work surrounding the large fireplace, the product of another insufficiently appreciated artist, Edward Maitland. Maitland had been a skilled ceramicist and interior designer, a craftsman who, if truth be told, was the muse to Morris's genius. Examples of his work could be found throughout the island, often unrecognised; there were several hotels with choice displays of his talent. An increasingly inebriated Dykes expanded upon his *bête noir*: the islanders' barbarous contempt for their heritage.

"The number of places," he declared, "where Maitland's tiling has been destroyed beggars belief. Painted. Whitewashed. Even chipped off the walls. Or whole buildings knocked down—the Belle View Hotel is a case in point—finest urinals in the land, it had. Razed to the ground! A Mace-Hopkins building, too! It's only because some bright spark on the council has woken up to the fact that heritage equals money that the whole damned lot hasn't been vandalised."

Dykes's indignation resonated with Sinclair, but a mild irritation at his companion's monopoly of the conversation made him play Devil's advocate. "What about the Electric Railway?" he interjected. "Surely that shows some respect? I'd have expected that to be closed down long ago. It can't possibly make a profit, can it?"

"The small matter of a successful lottery bid," replied Dykes, smiling. "Anything but fund it out of taxes! This place is riddled with obscenely rich tax exiles who resent every penny spent on culture."

Dykes reverted to his research. "There are supposed to have been seventeen buildings designed by Mace-Hopkins. There could have been more. No one here ever keeps proper plans or records. The island's archives are a disaster area. Some of the places I found just by driving round and looking. A lot of what I've pieced together comes from word of mouth. I've even spoken to an old couple on the island whose parents knew Mace-Hopkins. I can account for sixteen of the seventeen. There were four hotels. The Belle View. Then there's another been turned into offices. Gutted and the exterior defaced! The other two, oddly enough, were both destroyed in sensational fires in which guests perished, one in 1933 and the other in 1996. Of course, safety legislation over here is—how shall we put it—minimalist. Then we have the parish hall. That leaves eleven. All private dwellings. I've found ten of them. So the question is: where is the missing one?"

"Destroyed, maybe?" suggested Sinclair. "The island's not that big. Surely you'd have found it by now?"

"Maybe." snapped Dykes. "The trouble is, there are so many hidden corners in this place. Secluded mansions tucked away in woods. Big private estates you can't get near. There's one place owned by a Ukrainian banker. Electric fences. Dogs. And quite a few owned by criminals."

"Criminals or bankers, what's the difference?" slurred Sinclair, rising unsteadily to the bar as last orders sounded. They both laughed.

Sinclair returned with whiskies. "You see," Dykes continued, "there's a rumour that Mace-Hopkins designed a house for Maitland and his wife. It's definitely not one of the ones I've found—I've traced all their pedigrees conclusively. But it's known that Edward and Marianne Maitland lived on the island for a time. Their relationship with Mace-Hopkins wasn't just professional. Marianne's supposed to have had an affair with him before she met Edward. They were all into spiritualism. Marianne is said to have met Madame Blavatsky during her last months in London."

"All pretty scary, if you ask me." declared Dykes, "Marianne is supposed to have painted these weird pictures that outraged the salons of London and Paris. Inspired by visions, trances, automatic writing, visitations from angels and the Lord knows what else. Before she died—she killed herself, by the way—she had a lot of them destroyed. Now and again lost and unknown paintings crop up in auctions and private collections. She's supposed to have painted her best and darkest work during her final years— when she was over here." Dykes stared into his empty glass. "I sometimes wonder if there are any stashed away somewhere here on the island. It'd be just the place to find something like that. They'd be priceless."

Sinclair, stupefied by alcohol, listened. Marianne Maitland? Dykes's description rang a bell. "You mean Marianne de Lacey? The symbolist painter?"

"Of course," confirmed Dykes. "Maitland was only her married name. For professional purposes she always used her maiden name. She began as an apostle of the Pre-Raphaelites, and in my humble opinion did better than what they set out to do themselves. Her colours really shine, like the old Italian masters. Her command of the female form is unsurpassed. And there's something about the way she paints their draperies—you can almost hear them rustle."

"Absolutely!" said Sinclair. "*Truth Driving Falsehood from the Temple of Light*. The Walker Art Gallery, Liverpool."

"Right—an early work," said Dykes, "but weird enough. At first she tried to convey the idea of the triumph of light—all that Theosophical stuff—a kind of symbol for spiritual transcendence, the dawn of the afterlife and so on. But apparently the visions and the dabbling began to get her down. She had dreadful nightmares. Got depressed. Completely lost faith in the notion of light triumphant and began to see things in reverse, so to speak. They say that's why she destroyed her last paintings—and her life—too horrible a legacy."

)(

Next morning Sinclair felt depressed. What had seemed a good idea yesterday now felt foolish. Was there any point revisiting the cove? It would probably only make him miserable. But he had to do something with the day. At least it would be a trip on the railway.

He selected an open carriage, the better to imbibe the fresh morning air. The perspective across the sunlit sea was splendid. He marvelled at the intricacy of the coastline, the cliffs and crags where seabirds whirled and cried; and at the audacity that had driven an earlier generation to build this wonder in the wilderness. This half-forgotten railway was a masterpiece of engineering. It was strange how the extremes of rationalism and irrationalism met in the Victorian mind, the way bold, innovative technologies marched hand in hand with superstition and spiritualism.

Identifying the Grindle stop turned out to be harder than expected; few halts along the line bore station names. The young conductor looked blank when he asked for Grindle Glen. "Think I know where you might want," he opined. "There's an old footpath goes down to the shore. Just before Balmeanach. I'll give you a shout."

The tram had screeched to a halt before Sinclair realised he was there: there was no name, no platform, indeed nothing to suggest that it was even a stop. Sinclair searched in vain for any hint of the old entrance to the Glen. Thick shrubbery overhung the track. "Down there!" The conductor pointed. A narrow gap led through overgrown rhododendrons. This, presumably, was the Old Smugglers' Path. Apprehensively, he descended through the leafy tunnel.

The path widened as he proceeded, but it was not pleasant. Nettles and brambles choked the way. It was humid amidst the dense vegetation. Sinclair imagined he was having difficulty breathing. His head was aching. To his left the land plunged, impenetrably, through woods, where he presumed the Glen must lie. At one point where the thicket slightly thinned he thought he could see the roof of a building, but for the most part the empire of *Rhododendron ponticum* held unstinting sway. The path veered to the right, still steeply descending, brief vistas of the sea glancing through the foliage. A final awkward stumble over a grassy bank and he was there.

As is often the case, Sinclair's childhood Shangri-La looked much smaller and confined than he remembered. The huge, sharp-pointed rocks on which, Canute-like, he would defy the advancing tide, were in reality a few feet high. Though the exposed shore clearly indicated that the tide was at its ebb, the sea looked improbably near. The heathery cliffs which used to tower now seemed merely to enclose, and there were unsightly patches as if the headland had been burnt or was crumbling by degrees into the waves. Perhaps it was just the sultry weather, or his mood, but the cove emanated a lost, disconsolate, almost a menacing air. Everywhere was a universal drabness and the stink of rotting seaweed.

Sinclair took a few steps down the pebbly beach, thinking how awkward it was underfoot. He felt numb, emotionless, stunned by a bleak sense of anticlimax. But as he stood and stared it was as if the layers of the past peeled away. Through his mind, with the intensity of a mystic revelation, rushed myriad, heart-rending visions:

the crashing of the waves and their rustling retreat down the shingle; the pervasive scents of wild rose and honeysuckle, mingling with the bracing, brackish air; the litany of the swirling seagulls, like the voice of freedom; the indomitable power and euphoria of the lifeforce, when it had seemed that nothing in the world could die.

He surveyed the upper shoreline, seeking for the chalet. Miraculously, it was still standing, forlorn, ramshackle, bereft of paint. Stumbling forward on the slippery rocks, Sinclair saw that it was little more than a ruin; the walls survived and part of the roof; the verandah had long ago yielded to the elements. Within was still the familiar smell of sun-drenched wood. With a twist in his heart, Sinclair heard the sound of his mother's laughter, his father's reassuring voice. But otherwise there was only mockery. It was a tomb.

The emotions that swept over him, as he stood at last in this holy shrine, he could barely fathom. It was here, in this very place, that from a point of nothingness his existence in the universe had emerged, even as the universe itself, if the scientists were to be believed, had emerged from a singularity, a point of absolute nothingness—in what? Here, the world of form, of light and laughter, birds and trees and blooming, scented flowers, of joy and sorrow, indeed this very moment of reflection had been created— and created for Sinclair alone. Why? Vertigo possessed him as he contemplated the madness, the monstrosity of existence. Love, beauty, happiness. What were these? Would they all, then, return to nothing? Really, it was all a swindle.

Sinclair knew he had to leave.

It was some time before he realised he had missed the path. He paused to get his bearings, then saw the gate. It was rusted to immobility, folded back to its extremity against a collapsing fence. Lying on the ground was a rotting sign. *Private. Trespassers will be prosecuted.* Sinclair's memory stirred. He looked more closely: interwoven with the gate's vertical bars was a large letter G. G for Grindle. Here was the old exit from the Glen.

Curiosity impelled him. He pushed on through the open gateway into the heart of the woods; he could always turn back if it became impassable or encroached on private property. Despite the rhododendron mayhem the path was negotiable, and soon Sinclair was clambering alongside a series of waterfalls. Though the worse for age, a wooden handrail was still serviceable, as were the small bridges criss-crossing the stream. In the old days, he recalled, there had been fairy lights in the trees, allowing evening strolls as the summer nights drew in. And music in a bandstand. All the time the path was ascending.

Disliking the uneasiness of trespass, he was constantly alert for any sounds of activity ahead; but gradually he became aware that the focus of his wariness had subtly shifted. It was no longer directed so much ahead as behind, as if he feared pursuit. He paused, glancing back apprehensively. He was hot and enervated. The afternoon was still, airless, and once again he felt as if he could not breathe. Was that a rustling sound behind, like something bulky brushing through thick foliage? Or was it only the distant sound of the tide upon the shingle? There was certainly no breeze. Sinclair could have sworn he caught a higher movement in the branches of the trees above the rhododendrons; but as he peered behind and listened there was nothing. Be that as it may, he hastened ahead, abandoning any thought of going back on his footsteps. At least, he reassured himself, he was heading the right way; somehow or other he must surely reach the old front entrance.

Abruptly, he emerged into an area of open ground, very overgrown, like a lawn that had been left untended for years. The remains of low buildings and protrusions of twisted metal peeked through long grass. Recognition tumbled back, eerily clear: it was the area, not far from the entrance, that had contained a cafeteria, a children's playground and a maze. The old slide's rusting skeleton loomed up above unrecognisable debris, and the maze was a rampant glade of yew. Beyond loomed a substantial house. Sinclair had forgotten all about the house; but now, regarding it from across the slime-encrusted lily ponds, it was instantly familiar. But more than that: with a frisson of awe he recognised something he could never have been aware of as a child. Surely, here before him, amidst the wilderness and dereliction, practically in ruins, was Dykes's missing house, the one he had sought so fruitlessly, the very house Mace-Hopkins had designed for the Maitlands, the one, maybe, where Marianne de Lacey had taken her own life.

Mace-Hopkins's style was unmistakable: the delicate-angled, low-sloping roofs; the exquisitely proportioned mullioned windows; the graceful, curved entrance porch; the elegant chimney-stacks; the exquisite mathematical symmetry. Though shattered panes stared like vacant eyes, mildewed patches stained the once-white walls, and charred bare timbers spoke of past fire, it was evident to Sinclair that here the architect had reached the zenith of creation. This surely must have been his last design: it could never have been bettered. Sinclair could barely restrain his excitement. He would go directly that evening and tell Dykes. What sacrilege that this masterpiece had been allowed to fall into decay. Who on earth could be its landlord?

It was a disquieting thought. It brought him sharply back to earth. The sensation of being followed returned, now overwhelming; there was someone, he felt certain, coming up through the Glen. Again there were rustling sounds, vague movement in the trees. Anxious to remain unseen, he hastily circled the mansion. Outbuildings and low-level extensions indicated proximity to former stables and servants' quarters. A door hung open at the rear, teetering on a single rusting hinge. Cagily, he crossed the threshold. If anyone were wandering the Glen they would surely carry right on through; the house could not possibly be inhabited.

When his eyes adjusted to the shadows, Sinclair saw he was in a narrow corridor. Ahead was a staircase. Irresistibly, curiosity drew him on. Tentatively, he climbed the stairs, and came to a small landing. Before him was an open doorway. Beyond, extended a long, attic-like gallery, illuminated by stained-glass windows, still intact, which Sinclair, surprisingly, had not noticed from the garden. What he saw astonished him.

Ranged along each wall was a series of monumental oil canvases framed in a heavy, ornate gilt. Filtering beams of the late afternoon sun were palely sweeping the gallery, glancing across the paintings like a searchlight. There were maybe a dozen, and they were terrifying. The figures within them were greater than lifesize. With mixed sensations of dread and revelation, Sinclair knew, even before he looked more closely, what he had found. Here, hidden away from the world, even as Dykes had predicted, were surely the lost paintings of Marianne de Lacey, her final masterpieces, the ones she was reputed to have destroyed in revulsion at her own demented genius, before taking her own life. But they had survived.

There, in cynical parody of her own early work, was *Falsehood Driving Truth from the Temple of Light*. In *Oblivion Casting her Shroud over the Innocents* terror-stricken infants and nursing mothers scattered in dismay before a monstrous, robed figure in the louring skies. *Angel of Mercy* depicted a black-winged, hooded figure, clutched like a bird of prey onto a helpless maiden—what was so horrifying was not so much the fear in the victim's eyes but the astonishment. Sinclair wandered round in a delirium of horrified reverence, marvelling at the terrible beauty of de Lacey's inspired, nihilistic paintings, her last will and testament, the dreadful visions that had driven their creator finally beyond the edge. *Light and Beauty are Departed, The Anathema of Chaos, The Darkness Cometh and the Light Comprehendeth it Not, The Abduction of Persephone, For there is a Great Void, The Metamorphosis of Arachne, The Night of Time Far Surpasseth the Day and Who Knows When Was the Equinox?* The arcane titles blurred in his mind as he tried to comprehend the torment that had possessed this perverted genius. The terror of the subject matter was surpassed only by the devilishly skilful execution, and Sinclair could only wonder at the appalling nightmares and visitations that had inspired Marianne de Lacey's final creations. No one—not Goya, nor Salvator Rosa, nor Arnold Böcklin—had achieved such profundities of darkness.

There was one more canvas, larger than any of the others, commanding the full length of the gallery. It was as if it were all-important, the jewel in the macabre crown. The sun had gone and here the light was even poorer, as if the room were swathed in a greenish-grey mist. It was situated in a dim alcove.

Truly Dykes had spoken when he praised Marianne de Lacey's mastery of the female form, for the execution of the two foreground figures in *Nostalgia, Death and Melancholy* was exquisite. Melancholy was falling forwards, one long, elegant, bare arm thrust against her forehead, the epitome of inconsolable grief. Nostalgia was casting both her hands skywards, her face thrust back across her shoulder with a look of plaintive, harrowing anguish. Sinclair searched in vain for the third figure, which by rights ought surely to be occupying the centre ground. But there was only gloom. He thought for a moment it was an unfinished work, but decided that the artist's portrayal of nothingness was quite deliberate.

Sinclair drew nearer, but his concentration was broken by a sound coming from the other end of the gallery— from the direction he had entered. Too late he remembered his follower. He was gripped by a terrible foreboding. The magnitude of his folly overwhelmed him. He was trapped in a room with no other exit.

The sound was that of voluminous garments rustling, and whatever it was that was coming through the door must have been much too tall, from the way it stooped to negotiate the entrance.

Marie Emily Fornario:
A Historical Note

The strange case of Marie Emily Fornario as described in "M.E.F." is authentic. Miss Fornario came to Iona in the autumn of 1928 in search of spiritual peace, believing she had lived there in a previous life. She died in bizarre circumstances on the moors a year later. Her body was found in a hollow in the peat hacked out in the shape of a cross, with a knife lying beside her body. She was naked except for a black cloak. Her grave can be seen in the Reilig Odhráin, where ancient Scottish Kings lie buried, on the north side of St. Oran's Chapel, hard by the restored Iona Abbey. The tiny stone is in the form of an open book, inscribed thus: "M.E.F. Aged 33. Died 19th November 1929". Her tragic and macabre fate became embroidered over time, with increasing inaccuracy. The myth-making began right away with newspaper stories in the *Oban Times*, the *Glasgow Bulletin* and *The Scotsman*. They played up her link with occult circles in London, her eccentric behaviour, her strange appearance, the macabre nature of her death, as well as supernatural phenomena. The esoteric dimension was amplified by an article in January 1930 in *The Occult Review*—sufficiently careless of its facts to get her initial wrong as "N". Subsequent versions have tended to perpetuate the myth and obfuscate the facts.

Twelve years later Dion Fortune (Violet Firth) revived the case, making even more extravagant claims in her seminal study of occult phenomena *Psychic Self-Defence* (1942). Fortune was founder of the Fraternity of the Inner Light, member of the Alpha et Omega sect (formed by Mina Mathers), of the Hermetic Order of the Golden Dawn; and author of the occult detective volume *The Secrets of Dr. Taverner*. Fortune suggests that Miss Fornario, with whom she was "intimately friendly", was a frequent, reckless traveller on the astral plane; while on Iona she had become victim of a psychic attack—later alleging it had been by none other than the deceased Mina Mathers. Despite the appearance in 1955 of a more sober and accurate account based on first hand local evidence by renowned Scottish folklorist and travel writer Alasdair Alpin MacGregor, the more lurid story survived. Francis King's *Ritual Magic* (1970) and Peter Underwood's *Gazetteer of Scottish Ghosts* (1974) took their cue from Fortune. King reinforced *The Occult Review*'s mistaken initial, substituting Netta for Marie; and he inaccurately named the family she stayed with as MacRae, when it was Cameron. The truth was still further distorted in later populist accounts that played up the weirdness of Iona. Glasgow journalist Richard Wilson in *Scotland's Unsolved Mysteries of the 20th Century* (1995) repeated the inaccurate initial, citing her inscription as N.E.F. and naming her Norah; and also misspelling her surname as Farnario. Wilson renewed the erratic, though suitably weird, newspaper allegation that her body was discovered not amidst the moors but on the *Sithean* or fairy mound. In the most recent account from 2007, *The Guide to Mysterious Iona & Staffa*, TV producer Geoff Holder (maker of "Mysterious Scotland") reiterates the name Netta, even though the text has a photograph of the grave clearly marked M.E.F. Both writers acknowledge

King, Underwood and Fortune, but neither appear to have consulted MacGregor. Similar factual errors appear on internet sites.

Alasdair Alpin MacGregor was a meticulous chronicler of Hebridean lore who knew the people he was writing about. He respected their superstition and belief in the supernatural, germane to their culture. He wrote of the Fornario case in *The Ghost Book* (1955) in a chapter entitled "Haunted Iona". His account remains the fullest and most accurate, based neither on newspaper scandal nor on occult voyeurism, but upon conversations with local inhabitants, especially those who befriended Miss Fornario. A master of atmospheric prose, MacGregor tells a compelling ghost tale, but he also conveys the human tragedy: that of an eccentric, perhaps mentally disturbed loner who fell under Iona's disquieting spell; and of a community infused by awe and sadness at her terrible fate. The islanders told him of blue lights seen where she died and beside her grave. Some said they met her apparition wandering the moors. Alone of all the chroniclers, MacGregor tells that the two men who found her erected a small cairn where she died, indicating with fair precision the site: "between the Machar and Loch Staonaig, in a hollow on the chilly moor".

Who, then, was Marie Emily Fornario? She was, according to what the locals gleaned from her, the daughter of a wealthy Englishwoman and an Italian professor who taught at a university in Italy. Following her mother's death while still a child she grew up with an English aunt and uncle. She was estranged from her father, though he later claimed to have had a premonition of her death. She lived in affluent West London, Mortlake Road, Kew, and appears to have been well connected with a Bohemian set, which dabbled among more straightforward activities in the occult. Certainly, she was acquainted with Dion Fortune and the Fraternity of the Inner Light. She cherished a fascination with Hebridean lore as mediated by the fashionable writings of Fiona Macleod, pseudonym of William Sharp, who wrote in 1910 a study of Iona. (Supernatural author Margery Lawrence likewise mixed in these circles, dabbling with the occult and falling under Macleod's spell, illustrating a 1921 edition of *The Hills of Ruel*.) Miss Fornario's obsession with Macleod's Celtic fantasies is evidenced in her lengthy review, under the name Mac Tyler, of Rutland Boughton's opera *The Immortal Hour*, based on the poetry-drama of that name by Fiona Macleod.

This review (accessible on the website of the Servants of the Light School of Occult Science) offers fascinating insight into the state of mind of a woman drawn to Iona in pursuit of the mystical vision of Macleod. The review is an acolyte's appreciation more than a critical review, communicating great fervour. It is well written, albeit grandiose, displaying educated knowledge of the occult, spiritualism, mysticism and Celtic lore. What signally characterises it is the author's passionate identification with its theme, and with the heroine's epiphany. There is a scene in which the heroine, Etain, denies her suitor, Eochaid, who is imploring her to ignore fairy voices from the beyond. "I go from dark to light," she says. This, Fornario eagerly affirms, is the "Immortal Hour". The narrative is outlined and interpreted in obsessive detail, the composer's slightest deviation from Macleod's text neurotically noted, such as the omission of a "pregnant sentence": *There is no dream save this, the dream of death.* This, she asserts, implies that "death itself is only a dream" and that ultimate reality "lies in the other world, where all life is one life". It may be speculated that when Marie

Emily Fornario heard voices on Iona's moors, this is what possessed her mind. Did she that fateful night think she was passing over to the Light from the chilly moors of Iona? There is a further tale by Macleod that closely resonates with her fate. It concerns an old woman losing her daughter, Elsie, to the fairies. Elsie takes to visiting the moors by moonlight, fascinated by the haunted ruins of Dun Laraichean, and is last seen in the marshes by Loch Staonaig. Dun Laraichean is where Miss Fornario claimed to have witnessed apparitions and angels, and Loch Staonaig marks the scene of her death.

Marie Emily Fornario's experience on Iona is as described in "M.E.F.". Her secretive, eccentric behaviour at the farm; the candles kept burning at night; the blackened jewellery; the nocturnal visits to the moors; the physical and mental decay; the sudden urge to leave and its swift reversal; the talk of a terrible healing; the supernatural events following her death—all these were communicated by the islanders in talks with MacGregor. A strange part of the story is that, though on the night of her death Miss Fornario was barefoot, only her toes were bleeding, not her heels or soles, as a result of running over the heather: a curious circumstance that reminded MacGregor of medieval reports of saintly levitations. Marie Fornario was said by the islanders to have written mystical poetry, though none survives. Her own death became the subject of a poem by a Scottish writer, Helen Cruickshank, titled "Ballad of Lost Ladye". A fitting and poignant epitaph was expressed in a letter to MacGregor from Lucy Bruce who knew Miss Fornario well on Iona: "If you should be bringing her into any of your writings, please remember that she was a beautiful, gentle soul, full of loving kindness—a truly dedicated soul. Her strange and tragic passing moved us all."

In 2007 I went to Iona and, following MacGregor's clues regarding the location of the cairn, embarked on a search, exactly as described in "M.E.F.". As I was about to give up what was beginning to feel like a hopeless mission, I came suddenly upon a tumbled pile of stones. They rested in a hollow of the moor, very near Loch Staonaig, consistent with MacGregor's description. The discovery was preceded by a curious feeling of *déja vu* and an uncanny sense of a presence. It besieged me with the force of a revelation.

Sources

"Resurrection" first appeared in *All Hallows* #41, February 2006. It appears here with substantial revisions.

"Nostalgia, Death and Melancholy" first appeared in an earlier version in *Supernatural Tales* #11, Spring 2007. It appears here with substantial revisions.

"The Light of the World" was first published in *At Ease with the Dead*. Edited by Barbara and Christopher Roden, Ashcroft: Ash-Tree Press, 2007

"M.E.F." first appeared under the title "The Light Invisible, the Light Inaccessible" in *Cinnabar's Gnosis: A Homage to Gustav Meyrink*. Edited by Dan T. Ghetu, Bucharest: Ex Occidente Press, 2009

"Inheritance" first appeared under the title "Like Sisters" in *A Silent Companion*, Winter 2005. It appears here with substantial revisions.

"An American Writer's Cottage" and "A Midsummer Ramble in the Carpathians" appear here for the first time.

Acknowledgements

With many thanks to Barbara & Christopher Roden, David Longhorn, Katherine Haynes, Dan Ghetu, Bill & Jane Read, Keris Macdonald, and all members of the Everlasting Club; and to Ray Russell and Meggan Kehrli for the art and design, Jim Rockhill for proof reading, Laura Anzuoni for the Italian translations, and Brian J. Showers.

About the Author

Peter Bell has written articles and stories for *All Hallows*, *The Ghosts & Scholars M. R. James Newsletter*, *Wormwood*, *Faunus*, and *Supernatural Tales*; his work has also been published by Ash-Tree Press, Gray Friar Press, Side Real Press, The Scarecrow Press, and Hippocampus Press. Four collections of his stories have been published by Sarob Press: *A Certain Slant of Light*, *Phantasms*, *Revenants & Maledictions*, and *Sacred & Profane*; as well as a novella for *The Pale Illuminations*. Zagava Press have published *The Light Inaccessible*, reflections on his wanderings in the Scottish Isles. He has written introductions for Swan River Press collections by Henry Mercer and Katharine Tynan, and contributed to the anthology series *Uncertainties*. Bell is a historian, a native of Liverpool, an inhabitant of York, and likes to wander the hidden places of Scotland and the North of England.

SWAN RIVER PRESS

Founded in 2003, Swan River Press is an independent
publishing company, based in Dublin, Ireland, dedicated
to gothic, supernatural, and fantastic literature. We special-
ise in limited edition hardbacks, publishing fiction from
around the world with an emphasis on Ireland's contribu-
tions to the genre.

www.swanriverpress.ie

*"Handsome, beautifully made volumes . . .
altogether irresistible."*

– Michael Dirda, *Washington Post*

*"It [is] often down to small, independent, specialist presses
to keep the candle of horror fiction flickering . . . "*

– Darryl Jones, *Irish Times*

*"Swan River Press has emerged as one of the most inspiring
new presses over the past decade. Not only are the books
beautifully presented and professionally produced, but they
aspire consistently to high literary quality and originality,
ranging from current writers of supernatural/weird fiction
to rare or forgotten works by departed authors."*

– Peter Bell, *Ghosts & Scholars*

THE SEA CHANGE
& Other Stories

Helen Grant

In her first collection, award-winning author Helen Grant plumbs the depths of the uncanny: Ten fathoms down, where the light filtering through the salt water turns everything grey-green, something awaits unwary divers. A self-aggrandising art critic travelling in rural Slovakia finds love with a beauty half his age—and pays the price. In a small German town, a nocturnal visitor preys upon children; there is a way to keep it off—but the ritual must be perfect. A rock climber dares to scale a local crag with a diabolical reputation, and makes a shocking discovery at the top. In each of these seven tales, unpleasantries and grotesqueries abound—and Grant reminds us with each one that there can be fates even worse than death.

"A brilliant chronicler of the uncanny as only those who dwell in places of dripping, graylit beauty can be."

– Joyce Carol Oates

"Meticulously written and with carefully calculated chills."

– Black Static

NOVEMBER NIGHT TALES

Henry C. Mercer

Each story in *November Night Tales* is a differently coloured gem whose many facets reflect the lively mind of the author. Henry C. Mercer's life-long interest in world mythology, fairy tales, local legend, symbols, and artifacts form the fabric of his tales. Here, the reader will find vanishing castles, secret sects, biological weapons, sinister wilderness, lycanthropy, possessed dolls, and mythical lands. The characters in each story are driven to explore the unknown, face their fears, and perhaps discover something of themselves in the process. The compelling narratives, infused with intelligence and humanity, leave the reader curious why the stories remain virtually unknown today, and mournful that there are not more to explore. United at last with the six original November night tales is a seventh, posthumously published story, *The Well of Monte Corbo*. First published in 1928, this new edition is fully illustrated by Alisdair Wood and features an introduction by Peter Bell.

> *"While they might be over ninety years old, the tales feel fresh and modern in the way they address genre sensibilities, and Swan River are to be thanked for bringing this intriguing work back into print."*

> – *Black Static*

> *"The stories cover a wide range of themes exploring the various sides of dark fiction and displaying Mercer's many faces as a writer . . . a pleasant re-discovery of a neglected little gem from a not too distant past."*

> – *Mario Guslandi*

THE DEATH SPANCEL
and Others

Katharine Tynan

Katharine Tynan is not a name immediately associated with the supernatural. However, like many other writers of the early twentieth century, she made numerous forays into literature of the ghostly and macabre, and throughout her career produced verse and prose that conveys a remarkable variety of eerie themes, moods, and narrative forms. From her early, elegiac stories, inspired by legends from the West of Ireland, to pulpier efforts featuring grave-robbers and ravenous rats, Tynan displays an eye for weird detail, compelling atmosphere, and a talent for rendering a broad palette of uncanny effects. *The Death Spancel and Others* is the first collection to showcase Tynan's tales of supernatural events, prophecies, curses, apparitions, and a pervasive sense of the ghastly.

"Of remarkably high literary quality . . . a great collection recommended to any good fiction lover."

– Mario Guslandi

"Tynan's fiction is of a high standard, crafted in relatively simple yet still lyrical prose . . . a very assured craftswoman of the supernatural tale."

– Supernatural Tales

"Lovers of late Victorian and Edwardian ghost fiction will assuredly adore the restrained literary quality . . ."

– The Pan Review